Kisses Worth Waiting For

D1652061

YO - EGZ-399

Other Avalon Books by Lynn Bulock

LEAVE YESTERDAY BEHIND
THE PROMISE OF SUMMER
ROSES FOR CAROLINE
TALLIE'S SONG

KISSES
WORTH WAITING FOR

LYNN BULOCK

AVALON BOOKS
THOMAS BOUREGY AND COMPANY, INC.
401 LAFAYETTE STREET
NEW YORK, NEW YORK 10003

© Copyright 1991 by Lynn Bulock
Library of Congress Catalog Card Number: 90-93545
ISBN 0-8034-8852-1
All rights reserved.
All the characters in this book are fictitious,
and any resemblance to actual persons,
living or dead, is purely coincidental.

PRINTED IN THE UNITED STATES OF AMERICA
ON ACID-FREE PAPER
BY HADDON CRAFTSMEN, SCRANTON, PENNSYLVANIA

To Joe, for half a lifetime of love

and

In loving memory of Marguerite Haman Weaver, who with her husband, Fred, proved to me that love and marriage can last a very long time.

Chapter One

SHARON Turner lay stretched out on her back, trying to keep the sweat from dripping into her eyes. It was hot in the office, since the air conditioning wasn't working yet. Cousin Ed should take care of that by Monday. Right now Sharon's job was assembling this monster desk.

She brushed her short, dark hair out of her eyes and tried to concentrate on the odd little screws she was putting this hulk together with. Too bad the power screwdriver didn't have an attachment this size. She considered the picture she must present to anyone walking by—cutoff shorts, legs, and tennis-shoe-clad feet the only things showing while the rest of her wrestled with the underside of three hundred pounds of furniture.

Of course, her dad would have put this together for her. But she'd already asked him for so much help in getting this office set up. It wasn't fair for him to put in so many hours

2   *Kisses Worth Waiting For*

on his own business in Scott City, then drive up to Cape Girardeau every night and weekend to help her get this place open.

For a moment she considered asking Tanner for help; then she giggled. Garth Tanner Williams, attorney-at-law, might be her silent partner in this new business, but he wasn't about to get his hands dirty putting together the furniture. This was the man who'd needed intensive lessons to change the paper in the copy machine. There was no use trying to point him toward anything mechanical, not if she wanted it still standing when he was done.

Sharon felt around for another screw. Two more and the back of this unit would be on, and she could move on to one of the ninety-nine or so other jobs to finish before Shalimar, Incorporated, opened its doors next week.

There was the sound of footsteps crossing the carpet beside her, and Sharon could see dark trousers and well-shined shoes come to a rest next to the desk. "Excuse me, miss."

That was Tanner's voice, but there was a note in it she wasn't used to hearing. Hmm. The voice continued. "I was wondering where I could find— *Sharon?*" Tanner

Kisses Worth Waiting For 3

seemed amazed when she slid out from under the desk. "I didn't recognize— That is—"

"Didn't know I had legs, did you, Tanner?" Sharon said, an impish grin spreading over her face at the sight of Tanner standing over her, looking surprised. "That's because for the last four years they've been tucked under a desk typing your legal correspondence, polishing briefs, phoning clients. . . ."

"I get the picture, Sharon," Tanner said, his answering grin wry. "Limbs aside, I need a little help."

"If you haven't noticed, it's Saturday," she pointed out. "And if you haven't also noticed, you have a new secretary. I am now the proprietor of Shalimar, Incorporated, remember?"

"All too well. If I needed secretarial help, I'd go to your replacement, even if I do think she's too old, too methodical, and so forth. I'm not here to go over that ground again, Sharon. I need other help." Tanner almost looked sheepish. "Sarah Beth came with me this morning to move some books into my new office."

"That's nice. Does she want to come down here for a while and chat?"

4 *Kisses Worth Waiting For*

"She might, once you come up." There seemed to be something very interesting outside the window. Tanner's gray eyes seemed resolutely focused there.

"I really don't have time, Tanner. I've got to get this desk set up, and there are three smaller ones after this. . . ." Sharon trailed off. She'd seen that look before. Where his daughter was concerned, Tanner Williams went from a hard-nosed attorney to a teddy bear. "Okay, what's happened?"

"She's locked in the closet. Once she realized your office was on the first floor and mine was up on the third, she went into the supply closet and turned the key from the inside."

"Oh, nuts!" Sharon was heading for the door and up the stairs in the old Victorian house they'd lovingly converted to offices. Tanner was right behind her.

In his office it was cooler. The windows were all open, and here in the cupola of the grand old house, a breeze streamed through.

It probably wasn't very breezy in that closet. Sharon could imagine the solitary, stubborn little figure in there, probably sitting cross-legged on the floor, arms folded

Kisses Worth Waiting For   5

across her chest, glasses drooping off her short, freckled nose.

"Sarah Beth? I know you're in there. It's no fun talking through the keyhole, though," Sharon said, kneeling on the floor. "Why don't you come out where we can discuss this?"

"I'm not coming out. Not until you and Daddy agree to rethink your business arrangement," came a muffled voice inside the closet.

Any other nine-year-old would have said something real intelligent, like, "Make me," Sharon thought. But not Sarah Beth Williams. Sometimes she felt that the little girl was nine going on twenty-nine. Rethink their business arrangement, indeed. As if Sharon hadn't been rethinking it for almost four years just to get it to the point where it was now.

"It's a little late for that, Sarah Beth," Sharon said as gently as possible. "This is for keeps."

"But I didn't know you were going to be all the way down there." The voice was an honest, childlike wail now.

"It's not that far. And if you come out, I'll

6   *Kisses Worth Waiting For*

show you a secret." Sharon could almost hear Sarah Beth perk up.

"What kind of secret? A hidden panel in the wall? Ghosts in the attic?"

"Nope. Haven't found any of those yet. But there is an exclusive right of clients of Shalimar, Incorporated, who have fathers on the third floor of the building and best friends on the ground floor."

The closet doorknob turned, and the door opened a crack. "What kind of exclusive right?"

She had her now. Sharon had to fight to keep from crowing. "Come on, I'll show you."

Sarah Beth's bright-red head peeked out of the closet, and she slipped out, pushing her glasses up onto the bridge of her nose. "This better be good, or I'm going right back in."

But she followed Sharon out of the office, past Tanner, and out into the hall. "Look at this," Sharon said with a flourish.

Sarah Beth wrinkled her nose. "It's a plain, ordinary hallway and a plain, ordinary staircase."

"On the contrary," Sharon said, shaking her head. She leaned over to Sarah Beth, no-

Kisses Worth Waiting For

ticing with a pang that she didn't have to lean very far to whisper in her ear anymore. "It has a banister. Your banister, Sarah Beth Williams. The rest of us have to walk."

They shared a brilliant, conspiratorial grin, and then Sarah Beth gave a whoop and flung one mosquito-bitten leg over the banister and launched herself.

Tanner walked over to Sharon as they both watched her descent to the second floor, then the first. "Thank you," he said softly. "I never would have thought of that."

"If I thought it would hold my weight, I would have already tried it myself," Sharon admitted, watching Sarah Beth troop up the stairs for one more slide. "However, I suspect it would be beneath the dignity of a business owner, even a very new business owner."

They watched the girl go down again, giggling, and Sharon turned to Tanner. Even after all this time, looking into his face brought a leap to her heart that she had to push down before speaking.

"She really is welcome down there anytime, you know. I don't think that should change just because we're in different offices now," she told him.

8 *Kisses Worth Waiting For*

"I may take you up on that. I didn't realize how much being with you after school meant to her," Tanner said. "Here all these years I thought it was being near her loving father every afternoon that made her come straight from school to the office so quickly."

Sharon laughed. "It is, I'm sure. In a couple of weeks that banister is going to need polishing."

"Maybe, and maybe not," Tanner said. "I think Sarah Beth will keep it well shined all by herself."

Tanner was right on that score, Sharon reflected two weeks later. Every day Sarah Beth went into the building with a bang at three-thirty, climbed the stairs at lightning speed, and made Charlotte Mackelroy's life Hades on earth for about fifteen minutes.

Perhaps recommending Charlotte had been a mistake. But Tanner needed a nice, stable individual to run the office, somebody who didn't get flustered and who always knew where everything was. Trouble with Charlotte was she insisted on keeping things in their place all the time. And with Tanner there full-time and Sarah Beth there just fifteen minutes a day, that was going to be a losing battle for anyone.

Kisses Worth Waiting For   9

After fifteen minutes Sarah Beth had usually managed to get the office in an uproar and tell her father everything of interest about her day, and she'd zip down the banister to Shalimar, Incorporated. Maybe she wasn't always the perfect lady there, either, but then Sharon didn't expect her to be.

She saved big piles of the more obvious of the junk mail for her to open and sort and always tried to have some other little job that Sarah Beth could do. After a while she always found a snack, which Sharon usually shared. After all, four-thirty was quite a ways from lunchtime.

Once they'd unscrewed their sandwich cookies and drowned them in milk, or otherwise finished their gourmet delights, Sharon would settle Sarah Beth down in a corner to do homework while she finished up the business at hand.

Now if there was only more of that. Things were building. Sharon had to admit that. She'd been right a year ago when she'd tried to convince Tanner that there was a real need in town for a facility to support small businesses.

"Not everybody that needs one can afford a receptionist, a private office, secretarial

10 *Kisses Worth Waiting For*

help, and an attorney on retainer," she'd argued, watching his forehead crease. When she hit him with the idea to be the bankroll behind the scheme, he'd taken it well. It was only when he found out he was losing his own secretary that he balked at the idea.

"It's a great idea, really, Sharon. But do you have to actually run it? I mean, couldn't we just sell this great idea of yours to someone else . . ." he'd begun, using his best legal arguments.

It had taken six months of Sharon's using her own argumentative skills to get him to concede. Then it took five more months to hire her replacement. Only guaranteeing Tanner space in Shalimar's building and issuing an ultimatum had done it.

The ultimatum was that she'd quit, anyway, whether Tanner agreed to start Shalimar or not. And she'd meant every word of it. When they'd finally ironed out the details of building the facility with Mark Hagen this summer, Sharon had breathed a sigh of relief.

Not that Sharon was all that stubborn on most things, but here she had to draw the line. After four years of looking at the back, front, and sides of Tanner Williams and

Kisses Worth Waiting For   11

wondering if he was ever going to see anything but a secretary when he looked at her, it was time to move on. After all, she wasn't the green little girl straight from college anymore. Four years of working for Tanner had given her plenty of experience.

Experience enough to know that the tall, chestnut-haired lawyer was every bit the reality of her ideal man that she thought he was four years before. And experience enough to know that he was never going to realize that or care if he did. So it was time to do something else.

It was a little difficult to do, though. Even two floors below him, Sharon was still aware of Tanner. Aware of him when he whistled up the stairs every morning, leaving a little of the woodsy scent of his cologne in the hallway. Aware of him when he stuck his head into the office at least once a day to give her and her cousin Anna Mae Turner a hard time about something.

Even when Sharon had locked the door and driven home to Scott City at night, Tanner was still around. She couldn't go next door to Mama's for dinner without somebody asking about him. She couldn't sit home and read or watch television without

12 *Kisses Worth Waiting For*

thinking of something she wanted to tell him the next day. Sharon sighed, looking down at her too-neat desk. Like it or not, she was stuck with the image of Tanner Williams.

Now if she could only be stuck with a few more clients. For being open only ten days, business was encouraging. She'd had a few calls, and once that article the newspaper reporter came to interview her for came out, there would be more. If she could only get those two offices on the second floor rented, she'd be okay.

As if hearing her thoughts, a blond head poked in the doorway, followed by a tall, rangy body in a stiff new suit.

"Hi, stranger. Long time no see. What's new?" Sharon asked.

The young man's grin told her the answer, if the piece of paper he was flourishing didn't. "I passed the bar. Cape Girardeau's newest attorney is looking for an office, Sharon. Think you can help me out?"

"Only if you'd like to be on retainer for my other clients. At your regular fee schedule, of course."

After watching Jim struggle as Tanner's legal intern, then his clerk through the last

Kisses Worth Waiting For   13

year of law school, Sharon was prepared for the look of amazement on his face.

"Holy cow. I don't even have a regular fee schedule yet, Sharon. I don't even have a desk yet."

"Well, find one. And let me show you the office upstairs where you can put it, counselor." Sharon put an arm around his shoulders and led him off, listening to Anna Mae giggle in the background.

Jim was suitably impressed with the office. It was neat, clean, and had its own window, which was enough for him. Only when they were back at Sharon's desk reading the lease agreement did he turn a little pale.

"I really don't have a desk yet, Sharon," he said with a gulp. "So you can understand that I don't have any clients yet. Which means that once I've worked my way through my seed money, I don't know if I can even pay the rent."

"Come on, Jim." Sharon looked at him over the half frames of the reading glasses she locked away in a drawer when she didn't need them. "You have the recommendation of one of the most successful attorneys in town. And you'll do just fine on your own.

14 *Kisses Worth Waiting For*

So let's not worry about that for a while. I'm just starting out, too, remember?"

"It's hard to think of you as just starting out, Sharon. I mean, when I walked into the office not knowing a thing, you were the one who showed me the ropes. I think of you as an expert."

Sharon laughed. It was going to be refreshing to have Jim around again. "Thanks. I needed that. Now, why don't you go find yourself a desk?"

Jim nodded and left, visions of office furniture dancing in his head. He was carrying the list that Sharon had copied for him of where the best secondhand office things in the country could be had. Sharon knew that by Monday morning there would be a trailer outside filled with Jim's booty.

She almost envied him, starting out fresh and new in the sunny office upstairs, arranging his law books in neat rows and getting ready for his first independent client. Even though he was the same age she was, she felt light-years ahead of that stage.

Sharon glanced at her watch. It was almost time for Sarah Beth's daily assault. Maybe she'd pop some popcorn.

The smell drew even Tanner down the

Kisses Worth Waiting For   15

stairs. "Can I share your snack? I worked through lunch." His grin was so disarming, Sharon couldn't have turned him down if she wanted to. She arranged three chairs in the conference room.

After a few handfuls of serious popcorn, Tanner got into a contest with Sarah Beth to see who could flip the most kernels into their mouths without missing. Sarah Beth won. "Guess you're just getting too advanced for me, Peanut," Tanner said, ruffling her hair and standing up. "Well, I need to go back and finish up some loose ends before we go home. Coming, Sarah Beth?"

"Can I stay down here?"

Tanner looked at Sharon. "Sure," she said. "I've got a whole lot of envelopes to stuff."

"I'll collect her wages on the way out," Tanner told her.

Sharon and Sarah Beth both laughed as he left, and Sarah Beth rooted around for the last handful of popcorn in the bowl. "This is neat. It's almost like it was before."

"But not quite, right?" Sharon said, answering the wistful note in the child's voice.

"No. I still like it, though. That banister

16   *Kisses Worth Waiting For*

is neat. And it's fun being down here with you. There's always something to do."

Sharon picked up the popcorn bowl and the empty soda cans and went to get her stack of envelopes. She showed Sarah Beth how to fold the flyers announcing her open house in two weeks and stuff them into the envelopes. Sarah Beth went happily to work, rocking a little in the chair on wheels that she'd picked to sit in.

Sharon brought her own stack of correspondence into the conference room to sort through and keep her company. They worked in silence for quite a while, listening to the noises outside the window—traffic passing by and a few birds in the drowsy warm air.

When Sarah Beth started talking again, it was to regale Sharon with the latest goings-on in the fourth grade. The gerbil had escaped again, and this time it had taken three days to catch him. "He was in Marcie's desk, eating her math workbook," Sarah Beth said with a giggle. "Mrs. Grace said maybe it would make him smarter, but she hoped he didn't learn to multiply."

Sharon groaned at the bad joke. Sarah Beth finished the last envelope, licked the

Kisses Worth Waiting For   17

flap, and gave it a firm pat onto the stack of completed ones. "Now that I'm old enough to help around here, it's really neat. I don't have to make up my own games in the office to keep myself busy. I used to pretend that Dad's big partner's desk was a cave when he wasn't there sometimes. That was fun. And sometimes I used to pretend that you—" Suddenly she stopped talking and looked down. "Well, anyway, I'm older now, and I can help. Want me to sort these for the post office?"

"Sure," Sharon said, pretending not to see the flush on the child's face. She knew what Sarah Beth used to pretend when she was such a youngster, all of a few months ago: that Sharon was her mother. It had been so long since she'd had one that Sharon didn't mind her pretending that. It would have suited her just fine. But just like the cave under her dad's desk, it was pretend. And both she and Sarah Beth had better remember that, Sharon told herself. Life would be much easier for everyone if they both remembered.

Chapter Two

"So, Sharon, any progress with Tanner?" India asked.

Sharon gave her sister a grimace as she stirred banana bread. "No, not really. There isn't going to be, India. We might as well just face the fact that as far as Tanner Williams is concerned, I'm doomed to be an old maid."

India laughed. "There are many ways I'd describe you, Sharon. None of them are as an old maid. I just hope I'm as gorgeous as you are in four years."

Looking at her little sister, Sharon didn't see any indication that she wouldn't be gorgeous in four years. Now whether or not she herself was gorgeous was open to debate, but India, with her sparkle about everything she did and the quick, neat movements that complemented her slim figure and fall of dark hair, would be a beauty anywhere.

She saw India reaching toward the banana

bread. Sharon playfully smacked her hand with the spoon as she dipped a finger into the batter. "Enough of that. No sampling before it's baked. And no complimenting the cook in hopes that she lets you, either."

India smiled. "Just smoothing the top of this loaf. You wouldn't want it to come out of the oven all crooked, would you? Besides, if I were complimenting the cook, I'd have to say something nicer."

Now it was Sharon's turn to laugh. India swiveled on her stool and put her elbows on the kitchen counter. "And how come there isn't anything real nice to say, like commenting on your taste in fabulous guys? If Tanner Williams is history, or never was history, or whatever, Share, how come you aren't going after somebody else?"

There was a silence in the room, filled only by the low drone of the radio. Sharon shrugged. "Just not in the mood, I guess." It was hard to admit even to India that there was still a part of her that refused to give up hope. Somehow when she compared other guys to Tanner, they always came up short.

India broke the silence, finding it wise to change the subject. "Are you going with us

Kisses Worth Waiting For 21

to Mary Jo's birthday party? Kathleen's going to be there."

"Good. I haven't seen her since she moved back to town." Sharon slid both loaves into the oven.

"Yeah, and I figured you'd want to, anyway. You do know what she's doing now?"

Sharon shook her head as she loaded dishes into the dishwasher, and India looked pleased with herself to be passing on new information. "Public relations. She's been freelancing for some firm in Cape, but she says she'd really rather work for herself."

Sharon crossed the kitchen and hugged her surprised sister, almost knocking her off her stool. "Fantastic. Now I can fill that other office on the second floor. I ought to give you a commission."

"I'll take it in cash," India said, grinning. "There's a dress at the shop next to mine in the mall with my name on it."

"Now remember," Sharon told Kathleen as she checked up on her cousin in her office on Monday morning, "you don't need to tell Tanner right away that you're my cousin. After all, now that you're married, your last name isn't Mumford anymore, so he won't notice right away."

"So what's wrong with being your cousin, anyway? I've always liked being a Mumford." Kathleen tilted a pert blond head, studying Sharon. "In my business we believe in putting our assets first, remember?"

"It may be an asset to you and me, but Tanner's never been convinced there are that many Mumfords or Turners in three counties. He swears I just use this cousin thing as an excuse, sort of reverse nepotism or something for all the people I used to troop through his office and now troop through my own."

"Doesn't he have any cousins?"

"He's an only child of two only children. He doesn't even have aunts or uncles."

"Gee, the poor man. What does he do for entertainment without family gossip?" Kathleen went to the window, studying the view from her new office.

"He runs. And he plays with Sarah Beth, his daughter. Other than that, I haven't the slightest idea."

"I think it's silly, anyway," Kathleen said with a sniff. "I mean, when your mom is one of eleven kids and your dad one of nine,

Kisses Worth Waiting For   23

you're bound to have a lot of cousins. I bet you and India and Shane are the only ones in the family who have more cousins than I do. I mean, Dad had to go and marry somebody with only two brothers, so I'm at a disadvantage."

Sharon laughed. "You're going to be fun to have around, Kathleen."

"Yeah, and good too. I'm already bringing in four clients, including myself. I don't have a secretary, either."

"Great. Go introduce yourself to Cousin Anna Mae Turner, executive office assistant. She'll be glad to write you up a bill." Sharon ushered her through the door.

She looked around Kathleen's office one last time before she left. In only half a day Kathleen had transformed it into her own private space. There were broad-patterned ribbons holding back the staid curtains, and prints on the walls. A big bowl of potpourri filled with rose petals sat on the corner of the desk, next to a large brass frame with a picture of a smiling young man. That would be Matt, Kathleen's new husband.

Sharon knew that was the reason she'd moved back to town. Matt had been offered a job here better than the one he'd had in St.

24 *Kisses Worth Waiting For*

Louis, so they'd moved. And Kathleen was settling in just fine. Sharon pushed back a little surge of envy for her, with her life in order just the way she wanted it. Of course, it probably wasn't perfect from her side. Nobody's life was. But it sure looked nice from here. She straightened the frame of Matt's picture and went downstairs to see what India had packed in the lunch she'd left for her in the refrigerator in the kitchen. It was her week on kitchen duty. Sharon hoped she was out of her sprouts-and-tofu phase.

She was working out of it, anyway. There was actually some cheese in the pita-pocket sandwich along with all the nutritious shredded vegetables. Sharon found it hard to believe that this was the young lady whose favorite treat six months ago was a double cheeseburger with fries. And there was still banana bread left from Saturday, a nice slice to go along with the apple straight off one of Mom's trees in the backyard.

Sharon went into the conference room to spread her lunch out on the large table and look out the window. It had the best view of any room in the place except Tanner's cupola, and she could hardly eat lunch up there.

Kisses Worth Waiting For   25

She'd just gotten things spread out on a napkin when Tanner himself came in, carrying a bag from a fast-food place nearby. "Mind if I join you? I've got to be at the courthouse at two and just realized I hadn't eaten."

Sharon motioned beside her. That was Tanner, all right. Get him engrossed in the law, and everything passed him by, including lunch.

He sat down, stretching his long legs out under the table. Sharon wondered if he had to have his suits specially tailored. His shoulders were so broad and he was above average height, but so slender through the hips that he had to have those pants taken in. She pulled her concentration back to lunch instead of contemplating Tanner's suit measurements.

It was hard to do. Perhaps someday there would come a time when Tanner wasn't the most delightful thing to look at in the world, but Sharon couldn't imagine it. She'd felt that way almost from the moment she'd started working for him.

But back then he'd been a young widower trying to build a law career and raise a bouncy little girl at the same time, so she'd kept quiet. And slowly they'd drifted into a relationship where Tanner thought of her as efficient and helpful and friendly, but certainly not serious dating material. It was a little late in the game to change that now.

Tanner finished his sandwich and crumpled the wrapper into a ball. "I keep meaning to ask you if you know a good carpenter. I've decided I really want to build shelves into that one wall of the office."

"The one I said would look so nice with shelves?" Sharon asked sweetly.

He grinned. "That's the one. Got any idea?"

"Well, there's my dad, but he does mostly cabinetry these days, or Cousin Sid Bradley. . . ."

"Bradley. Now there's a new addition to the infamous cousin roster," he teased.

"His mom's a Mumford," Sharon said almost absentmindedly. "No, I've got the perfect person." She got up and stuck her head out the conference-room door to talk to Anna Mae. She came back, smiling. "Paul Turner. Excellent carpenter and excellent references."

"Naturally, being a Turner. A cousin, no doubt."

Kisses Worth Waiting For   27

"Of course. Anna Mae's brother. He usually works in construction, but he had an accident and has been off awhile. He's about ready to get back to work. I know he'd do a perfect job, Tanner. Want me to arrange it for you?"

"As long as I get to meet this particular 'cousin' sometime before the final work is done so he knows just what I want."

"I've got a fair idea, but I'll make sure Paul talks to you before a board is touched."

Tanner stood up, smiling. "Thanks. Now I've got to get to court. If Hurricane Sarah Beth comes in before I get finished, keep her down here, okay? I don't think Charlotte's up to her alone."

"That's putting it mildly."

"Is she okay when she's down here?"

"I haven't had to replace anything that cost over a hundred dollars," Sharon said. She watched Tanner's forehead wrinkle with anxiety. "No, seriously, she's fine, Tanner. You know that she and I have always gotten along well."

"You have," he agreed. "Tell her I'll be back by four-thirty at the latest unless this is far more complicated than I expect. Tell her it's a probate case. She'll understand."

28   *Kisses Worth Waiting For*

"Will do," she said cheerfully, watching him straighten his tie on the way upstairs. Sarah Beth would understand probate too. She'd learned to read out of her father's law books and had more familiarity with Blackstone than with Barbie dolls. Once in a while Sharon wished she could change that.

She'd haul her out to the country and throw her on a horse with the rest of the kids, or get her swinging on her mom's old willow tree. Or any one of a number of other things she knew Sarah Beth would enjoy. Maybe she'd ask Tanner sometime if she could borrow her for the weekend. It would be fun to have her.

Sharon cleaned her few crumbs off the conference table and went back to work. The first thing she did was call Paul, who was delighted to have the job. She set up a time the following week when she could introduce him to Tanner.

That done, she went up the stairs to Tanner's office to have Charlotte put a reminder on his desk calendar.

"Why don't you go in and do it?" Charlotte asked. "He says my handwriting is harder to read than yours." Her voice held a note of injury. Sharon suspected that Char-

Kisses Worth Waiting For 29

lotte had heard plenty about the way she'd run the office.

Not that it had been so wonderful. It was just that she'd had a way of anticipating Tanner's requests and caught on quickly to the way he liked things done. It had been fun working for him, learning the intricacies of the law and the intricacies of the person there.

Some of them she'd never unraveled. After five years there was still a picture of his wife on his desk, a small head-and-shoulders portrait of a woman with deep, burnished red hair. Across the desk was a large double frame filled with last year's school picture of Sarah Beth and a picture she'd drawn him. The portrait of Sarah Beth made Sharon smile every time she saw it, and the other photograph made her heart sink.

If these were the things Tanner still held most dear, it wasn't much use trying to press any kind of relationship. Sarah Beth had been just old enough to have memories of her mother, and from what she'd told Sharon, Sharon had found it impossible to think about competing.

Other than the pictures, the office was all business. The green-glass lamp on the desk

30   *Kisses Worth Waiting For*

and the leather blotter were so sedate. They matched the heavy, dark-striped wallpaper he'd insisted on above the chair rail. It had the solid look of an office for a much older man about it, but that was what Tanner wanted, so that was what Sharon had installed.

The bookcases would look good in the corner where he wanted them now. Of course, she had planned to have them built in originally, but Tanner had balked at the cost. So she'd decided to wait until he missed them to add them in.

Sharon leaned over the desk and flipped the calendar to Monday. She used Tanner's pen to write in his appointment with Paul, putting a reminder about who he was after his name. That way Tanner would have no excuse to look up from his desk, all owl-eyed, when she ushered her cousin in. There would be no way he could say this time that she hadn't told him about something in advance, when in reality he'd gotten so involved in research for some case that an entire circus full of elephants could march through the office and he wouldn't know.

And then there was Sarah Beth, who typically marched in like the herd of elephants.

Kisses Worth Waiting For   31

It wasn't any different today when the door flew open and she and her book bag came careening in.

"A new girl came into our class today. She just moved here and her name's Ginger and she wants me to come home from school with her on Thursday. Do you think I can?"

"Up to your dad, my friend," Sharon said briskly. "He'll be here as soon as he gets back from court, and you can ask him then."

"Okay," Sarah Beth agreed, somewhat deflated.

"Anna Mae brought in brownies this morning. I saved you two," Sharon told her. "Go back to the coffeepot, and you'll see them, wrapped in foil."

Sarah Beth nodded and headed for the kitchen. When Sharon went to check on her later, she'd finished her snack, cleaned up the crumbs, and was working on her homework. Going to Ginger's had to be very important to merit this much sterling behavior.

When Tanner came back, he'd gotten halfway in the doorway before Sarah Beth found him. "Whoa, slow down," he said, trying to stop the verbal onslaught with an upstretched palm. "Now, take a breath and start over. Who is this Ginger, and where

32   *Kisses Worth Waiting For*

does she live? Will one of her parents be home on Thursday, and how long does she want you to stay?"

Sarah Beth fired off all the answers to his questions and stood, balancing from one foot to another. "Well?"

"I can't see why you couldn't. I might want to call Ginger's mother and see if Thursday is really convenient for her."

"Spoken like a true lawyer, Tanner," Sharon said, watching the puzzlement on the girl's face. "Anybody else would have just said maybe."

"So I'll go upstairs and call now. Will that suit you two?"

"Yes!" Sarah Beth nearly exploded. "I've got Ginger's number in my book bag. Let me come with you."

Tanner loosened his tie as he headed for the stairs. "Court was fine, thank you. The probate went smoothly, and my client was very pleased. If anybody cares," he said pointedly, an eyebrow raised in Sharon's direction.

"Okay, so you didn't get a hero's welcome. So we're all glad to see you, Tanner. It's never any other way."

Sharon's answer seemed to take him by

Kisses Worth Waiting For   33

surprise. He turned on the first stair of the staircase and looked back at her. "I'm happy to hear that. Thanks." He still wore an air of puzzlement, much like Sarah Beth's, as he climbed the stairs.

At least Sharon's preparation paid off and Tanner didn't look puzzled when she and Paul walked into his office the next week. He stood up from the sheaf of papers spread over the desk and shook Paul's hand, even called him by name. The two of them seemed to hit it off right away, and Sharon breathed a sigh of relief.

"I'll be down in my office," she told them both as she headed for the door. "Stop by after you're done for a cup of coffee, cousin."

"Will do." Paul was already sketching something on paper and getting out a rolling metal tape measure. There was a gleam in Tanner's eye when she called Paul "cousin" that made Sharon want to stick her tongue out at him, but she refrained.

By the time Paul was coming down the stairs, Sharon had cleared her own desk off for the third time that morning and was ready for a cup of coffee. She poured them both one and motioned for him to sit down.

34   *Kisses Worth Waiting For*

"So how's life at your end of the world?"

"Rough but getting better," he said, running a hand through dark-brown hair and sitting down. "I'm just starting to get out from under the bills from this back problem, being off work for so long. Hopefully we'll get them all paid off before the baby comes."

Sharon nodded. "December, right?"

"Far as we can tell. And I think we're going to have to take Buddy in to the doctor if he doesn't get better." His face clouded as only a devoted father's can, and Sharon saw his active two-year-old in her mind.

"Oh?"

"Yeah. I don't know whether he's just imitating the old man walking a little sideways, but I swear he's limping. I told Kay we're giving it a couple more days, and then we're taking him in to the doctor. I'll even go with her so she doesn't look like an old mother hen."

"Good for you," Sharon said, giving his shoulder a squeeze. Paul had always been one of her favorite cousins out of the mob of kids around her age who had grown up together. He was quiet and thoughtful and lots of fun to be around. Almost as much a brother to her as her own brother, Shane. "So how about another cup of coffee?"

Chapter Three

SHARON sat at her desk, doing the monthly statements for all her accounts. It was nice to have enough of them to keep her fairly busy now. There were twelve clients for Shalimar, all using some kind of small-business services, if you counted Kathleen and Jim. It was a pleasant kind of feeling to know she'd been right about the area needing small-business services.

Now if she'd only been right about Tanner. She'd hoped that absence, at least the kind that having two floors separating them provided, would make his heart grow fonder. He ate lunch with her regularly, and they discussed Sarah Beth and her goings-on, but that was about it.

Otherwise there was no difference in the way Tanner reacted to her. After that day he'd found her putting together the desk, Sharon had thought there might be. He'd showed honest surprise that there was a

36 *Kisses Worth Waiting For*

woman where his secretary had been, it had seemed. However surprised he'd been, though, Tanner was still his staid, business-like self.

Sharon sighed. She needed one more file to finish the monthly statements, and where was it? As she traced her movements of the last few hours and the evening before, it came to her. The folder was on the seat of her car, out in the parking lot. She got up from her desk and stood, thinking. Should she close up the windows? Not for just the minute or two she'd be out there, even if she was the only one here. The Indian-summer breeze coming in felt too good to shut out.

Besides, in a moment she'd be back at her desk. Tanner would have snapped at her about security and all that, but he wasn't here, so he didn't have to know. Sharon got all the way to her door before she realized that her keys were still on the desk. That was no good. She couldn't get into the car without them. She turned in the doorway to go back when the gust of wind came through the windows, pushing the heavy oak door toward her.

These old houses were built to last. It was a quality that had made her choose this place

Kisses Worth Waiting For   37

for Shalimar in the first place. It was also
something Sharon felt like cursing right at
the moment. A lighter door would have
yielded to her touch. A lighter door wouldn't
have eaten the hem of her skirt, either. Now
she was stuck.

She looked at her watch. Seven forty-five.
Nobody else would be coming in for at least
forty-five minutes. Even when they did come
in, she might be stuck here awhile. There
were only two master keys for all the office
doors, one on the key ring sitting on her
desk, and one in Tanner's possession, probably locked methodically in the drawer of the
big partner's desk upstairs. And, knowing
Tanner, he kept the only key for the desk
drawer all to himself. As little as he was
pleased with Charlotte Mackelroy, chances
were good that she didn't have duplicate
keys.

For a moment Sharon almost cursed her
own practicality. Usually she prided herself
on it, but right now she wished she were a
little less practical. If she were, maybe the
full skirt of her favorite crimson dress
wouldn't have been made of such sturdy material. Then she could have yanked it out of
the closed door.

38 *Kisses Worth Waiting For*

No such luck. She was trapped here, and she couldn't even sit down. The wind had caught her dress at such a level that her only option was to stand here, leaning against the door perhaps, until somebody came along. Rats!

Sharon spent the time thinking about how she was going to get out of this mess. If Anna Mae were the first one in, she could send her around the building to shinny in the window of her office and retrieve her keys. Of course, Sharon would owe her for it, and her misadventure would be the talk of the next family reunion, but it would be worth it. If Charlotte were the first in, she could tell her the secret of jimmying Tanner's desk drawer with a paper clip. He'd probably skin her if he ever found out, but it would be better than him finding her trapped in a door.

Sharon perked up her ears. Somebody was coming in the front door. Someone who rattled keys and took a while to cross the hall. "Hey," she called loudly. "Come in here, whoever you are. I'm stuck."

"You certainly are." Tanner stood in the office doorway, grinning. He had a cup of coffee, still steaming through the lid, in one hand and a bag that smelled suspiciously like

Kisses Worth Waiting For   39

cinnamon rolls in the other. "Would you care to explain this?"

"Not particularly. Would you care to get me out of here?"

"I suppose. It's kind of interesting just watching. I ought to find a camera. The reading glasses make a particularly attractive touch, Sharon."

"Arrgh! I'd forgotten I had them on. Tanner, stop standing over there grinning and get me out of here."

"Certainly." He put his breakfast down on Anna Mae's desk and strolled over, surveying the situation. "Maybe we can just slide you out of there. . . ." Tanner stood on one side of her and then the other, looking.

"I doubt it—" Sharon began, then stopped. Tanner stood behind her, reaching one way and the other, trying to find a polite way to get a handful of her skirt. Finally he reached around her, one arm on either side, and grasped the material.

Sharon fought a sharp intake of breath. Maybe this wasn't going to get her loose, but she sure hoped Tanner tried for a while. They were close enough that she could smell his fresh cologne, almost feel his chin graze the top of her head. Tanner had his arms

40   *Kisses Worth Waiting For*

around her, strong arms encased in half-soft, half-prickly gray-flannel suiting. After a good yank on the cloth he leaned back. "Not going to work, is it?"

"Don't think so," she said slowly. "Of course, if you want to try again, you could."

"I might." He leaned into her again, and she closed her eyes. Here it was, what she'd fantasized about for years, and all so innocent it hurt. Tanner would never know what this was doing to her.

And again maybe he would. He had stopped pulling on her skirt, trying to free it, but he was still there. He was there, his lips grazing her neck, murmuring something soft she couldn't understand. When she turned her head to see if that was really him, if this was really happening, he was still there.

The kiss surprised her, captured her in a warm, deep wave. Tanner's lips were warm and tasted of the one sip of coffee he'd stolen from that cup sometime before he came in. They were infinitely sweeter than Sharon had ever imagined, and she shivered with the pleasure of them as she put one hand softly on his shoulder.

That broke the spell. Tanner suddenly

Kisses Worth Waiting For   41

straightened, gray eyes startled. "The key's up in my desk drawer. I'll go get it."

Sharon stood, confused, feeling bereft. What had happened? She touched her lips and could still feel the imprint of Tanner's there.

When he came back, she was as business-like as she could expect to be with one side of her skirt locked in the door. He handed her the key and retrieved his breakfast. She unlocked the door, got her own keys, and handed his back with a murmured thank-you. And that was that. Tanner seemed very careful not to touch her, only the keys, and Sharon followed suit. She fought to keep the tears from stinging her eyes as she walked out to the car for the file.

At ten o'clock that morning, when Charlotte called and asked her to come up for a little meeting with Tanner, all the way up the stairs Sharon rehearsed what she would say. She didn't want to apologize exactly, because she was far from sorry. And whatever happened, she felt it hadn't been her fault, anyway. All she'd wanted was to be rescued from a clothing-eating door, but she'd gotten much more than that. Tanner, after all, was the giver.

His opening words flustered her so much she never got her carefully prepared speech past her lips.

"I'm really sorry about what happened this morning. I made a total fool of myself, and I'd appreciate it if you kept it to yourself, all right?" He sat behind his desk, protected by his barrier of paperwork.

"Of course," she said through tight lips. "Was that what you called me up here for?"

"Not exactly. I just figured I couldn't ask you anything until I cleared the air."

Some clearing. Sharon felt as if the air were settling around her like a thick fog. So kissing her had made Tanner feel like a fool. Thanks heaps, Tanner. "What was it you wanted to ask me?" she managed to get out.

"Well, it's kind of a personal favor," he began, looking uncomfortable.

A personal favor. Oh, great! The man who got embarrassed touching her now wanted to get personal. Maybe he was out of postage stamps or something. Sharon forced herself to look polite and interested. "Go on."

"Well, you know I've got that ABA weekend coming up in Kansas City. I figured it

Kisses Worth Waiting For   43

would be really easy to find someone to watch Sarah Beth. In fact, I had everything all set up with Ginger's mother that she'd just stay there for the weekend. But now there's a hitch in the plans." He stopped, looking at the ornate trim of the ceiling. "Ginger, it seems, broke out in chicken pox this morning."

"Which Sarah Beth has not had."

"Correct. And even if she had, I could not expect a woman who already has one whiny, itchy nine-year-old on her hands to take on another healthy one."

"So you need a place for her to stay for the weekend."

"Exactly. I was wondering if in that file of . . . er . . . 'cousins' of yours, you had any reliable sitters."

"Garth Tanner Williams!" Sharon exploded, standing up and leaning on her desk. "Why can't the child just pack her suitcase and stay with India and me? We'd be pleased to have her."

"With you? You'd take her for the weekend?"

"Anytime. I was thinking of asking you if she could come out while the weather was still nice, anyway. My aunt's keeping a pony

44 *Kisses Worth Waiting For*

at Mom's right now for some of her grand-kids, and the apples are in. We'll have a wonderful time."

Tanner smiled, looking a little dazed. "I'm sure you will. I'll tell her to pack."

Sarah Beth had packed enough in her bulging suitcase to last at least a week. Sharon stifled a laugh, watching her drag it across the office parking lot. Then she helped her hoist it into the trunk of her car and watched as she kissed her father good-bye. She seemed impatient for Tanner to leave so the fun could start. Before he was finished giving her instructions on how to behave, she was in the car, seat belt on and ready.

Sharon handed Tanner the homemade map that showed him how to get to her house on Sunday. "Don't worry. I'll take good care of her."

"I'm sure you will. She's got all my emergency numbers in her suitcase, along with everything else," Tanner said, straightening his tie. He leaned in the open window of Sharon's car and kissed Sarah Beth again. "Be good, Peanut."

"Oh, Daddy, I will be," Sarah Beth insisted. "We'll see you later."

Kisses Worth Waiting For   45

"Gee, and I'll miss you too," he said wryly. "Have a good time."

Sharon laughed. "Be glad she's not homesick. That would be worse."

"I guess so. But I'm already thinking about what kind of tools I'm going to need to pry her away from you on Sunday. I don't think a crowbar and a jack handle will do it, and that's all I've got in the car."

"We'll think of something," Sharon promised, getting into the car herself. "Good-bye, Tanner."

Sarah Beth chattered all the way to Scott City and bolted out of the car the minute it stopped in the driveway. "Where's the pony?"

"Probably in his stall, unless Missy and Mike are riding him."

"Can I go see?"

"Sure. Just cut between the two houses here and head toward the back, over there." Sharon pointed the way.

Sarah Beth didn't have to be told twice. Her legs fairly flew in the direction of the small stable at the back of the property. Sharon got the suitcase out of the car and took it in to the upstairs bedroom of the little house.

46   *Kisses Worth Waiting For*

Setting the suitcase on the bed, Sharon looked around. India had done a good job getting their guest quarters ready, simple as they were. She had dug through a trunk in Mom's attic and come up with some stuffed animals and dolls that had been theirs years ago. And there on the small bedside table was Sharon's ancient, battered copy of *Little Women.* That sure brought back memories. She could see herself, sprawled across a bed, about Sarah Beth's age, reading the book. It was going to be fun having her here.

Sharon heard a whoop and looked out the window. Missy and Mike had the pony out and Sarah Beth on top of it, cheering her on. It appeared to be her first pony ride, judging from the wobbling, but the other two were keeping her going.

"I only fell off once," Sarah Beth exclaimed when Sharon came to get her for dinner. She rubbed a muddy spot on her jeans to prove it. "Isn't even sore anymore."

"Great. Come wash up and have dinner. Horseback riding is hungry work."

"You can say that again." Sarah Beth skipped into the house after Sharon.

That evening Sarah Beth discovered the stack of books on the bedside table. She

Kisses Worth Waiting For   47

started *Little Women* at once and was still engrossed when Sharon came to tuck her in later. "This is neat up here," Sarah Beth said. She had pulled a chair up to the windowsill, where the second-story window opened onto a huge oak tree. "Almost like having my own tree house or something. Sharon?"

"Yes?"

"Is this house yours?"

"Well, India's and mine, for now. It belonged to my grandma, and she left it to my mom, and Mom lets us live in it."

"So if you . . . got married or anything, would you still live here?"

"No, I expect I would go live wherever my husband did," Sharon said carefully.

"Oh." Sarah Beth was quiet for a minute. "But this house would still be here."

"Sure would. And India loves company." Sharon ruffled Sarah Beth's hair. "Besides, I don't have any plans to get married or anything, anyway."

"That's too bad," Sarah Beth said with a smile, settling onto the bed. "I've always wanted to be in a wedding, and we're such good friends, I know you could use a junior bridesmaid or something."

48   *Kisses Worth Waiting For*

"Don't hold your breath, kiddo. But thanks for the offer. Lights out in ten minutes, okay?"

"Okay."

Sharon went downstairs and picked up her own book. She could remember when her grandmother still owned the house. As a child, sleeping over in that room that had reminded her, too, of a tree house. She tried to remember what it really felt like, going back that far, but it was a little fuzzy. She wished she could find the right words, the perfect, gentle words, to make Sarah Beth realize that nothing more was ever going to happen between her and Tanner.

Sharon sighed. To find those words, she'd have to believe them. And she didn't yet, not all of her. After Tanner's kiss it was harder than ever to believe. But still, the practical side of her argued, four years was a long time to be just friends. If something else was going to happen, it would have by now. Sharon could hear Sarah Beth padding across the floor, switching off the light. She opened her book and tried to find her place.

Saturday passed in a blur of activities. Sharon and Sarah Beth baked cookies, and

Kisses Worth Waiting For 49

Sarah Beth taught Missy a few new tricks in tree climbing and got better at riding the pony. That evening they had supper at Mom and Dad's, everybody laughing and talking around the big dining-room table. Sarah Beth's eyes shone. She enjoyed all the goings-on, especially Shane's teasing her. He was nineteen and loved every minute of having her and Missy to tease. Sharon didn't mind, as long as it was friendly. At least it gave her and India a break, for a change.

Sarah Beth enjoyed her bath in the old claw-footed tub. Sharon could hear her singing in among the bubbles for quite a while, bouncing quite a concert off the tile walls of the bathroom. When she came out in her nightshirt, she hugged Sharon tightly before she went up to bed. "This was a great day. I like being an only child okay, but it would be neat to have a family too. Thanks for sharing yours, Sharon."

"Anytime," Sharon said, hugging her back. "Let's see if we can talk your dad into letting you do this once in a while, okay?"

"Okay!" Sarah Beth nearly floated up the stairs.

Sharon went into the kitchen to get caramel rolls put together to rise in the refrigera-

50 *Kisses Worth Waiting For*

tor for breakfast. Might as well make Sarah Beth's last day here extra special. Sliding the rolls into the refrigerator, she paused. There was something happening upstairs.

Sharon climbed the stairs and listened at the door. There was a muffled sound, like sobbing, coming from Sarah Beth's room. Sharon knocked, then went in. "You okay?"

"No," Sarah Beth said, looking up with tearstained cheeks. "She's dead."

"Who, sweetheart?" Sharon asked, coming to wrap her arms around the child on the double bed that suddenly looked huge.

"Beth. In my book. Why did she have to die, Sharon? Why does anybody have to die?"

Sharon held her while she burrowed into her shoulder and let her cry it out. "I don't know. I wish I did, and then I could tell you. But I don't." Sharon looked at her helplessly. So this was what real parenting was like. Ouch. She had new respect for Tanner.

In a little while Sarah Beth calmed down, using the back of her hand to wipe her cheeks. "Thanks," she said, hugging Sharon. "I'll be okay now."

"Sure? If you need me, just holler. I'll be right downstairs."

Kisses Worth Waiting For 51

"I'll remember," Sarah Beth said.

"Good." Sharon went to sleep half expecting a call in the night, but none came. In the morning Sarah Beth was cheerful again, competing with India to see who could devour more caramel rolls. At three they called it a tie and offered to clean up while Sharon showered.

"Today we pick apples," Sharon announced, coming out into the living room. "Everybody ready?"

"Anytime," Sarah Beth said, looking up from the checkers set she and India had set up. "We were just waiting for you. How come you take so long in the bathroom, Sharon?"

"You should see all the stuff she keeps in there," India told her. "Moisturizer, hair stuff—three different kinds—and then there's the makeup and the cologne. It takes her all day, Sarah Beth."

Sharon made a face at both of them. "Just wait until you get as old as I am. You'll take forever to put your face together too."

"I hope not," India said. "I've got better things to do with my time. Your move, Sarah Beth."

India lost at checkers, the first time in

52 *Kisses Worth Waiting For*

months. Usually she beat Shane or Sharon handily, but Sarah Beth was an expert. "My dad plays chess with me. Do you play chess?"

"No," India said, "but Dad does. Maybe next time you're out, you can play him. Right now I think we need to go out to the orchard before Sharon wears a spot in the floor tapping on it. What do you think?"

Sarah Beth cocked her head, grinning. "Could be. Is she always this impatient?"

"Not all the time," India told her, grabbing her hand and heading for the front door. "Sometimes she's worse."

Sharon chased them both into the orchard. The air was crisp and cool, with sunshine filtering between the trees. She looked for the perfect apple to eat while she picked and found it, huge, red, and crisp.

Sarah Beth laughed. "You have apple juice running down your chin."

Sharon used her free hand to snap an apple off a twig and toss it to Sarah Beth. "You will, too, in a minute."

In the afternoon Mrs. Turner brought out platters of sandwiches and cookies, and Shane came to help pick. "This is the biggest crop yet, Mom. What are we going to do

Kisses Worth Waiting For   53

with all of these apples?" Sharon asked, sprawled in the shade of a tree.

"Besides make a few dozen pies for you and Shane, and give a bushel each to your aunts who've asked for them, and make apple butter and. . . ."

Her mother was still ticking things off on her fingers when Sharon stopped her, laughing. "Never mind, I get the picture. And after lunch I get the ladder, India. You can do the lower branches with Sarah Beth for a while."

"Fine. She doesn't eat more than she picks," India teased. "You've probably eaten enough apples to keep the doctor away until November, Share."

"So I'll slow down after lunch."

After lunch Sharon took her place on the ladder. There was a breeze in the branches of the trees, and slow, buzzing bees hummed around her. She could hear India and Sarah Beth laughing and talking below her. Once in a while she called to Shane, who would replace the basket she had filled with a new one.

In the warm quiet of the afternoon, Sharon hummed to herself. She had a full basket again and could hear Shane behind

54 *Kisses Worth Waiting For*

her. "Help me down with these, will you?" she asked. "I need a break from the top of this ladder."

"Don't mind if I do." The voice was several registers lower than Shane's, and the arms around her waist lifting her down from the ladder were different too. Sharon turned around once she got to the ground. It was Tanner, but a different Tanner than she'd ever seen.

This man wore a faded chambray shirt and blue jeans, and a smile that seemed to go with his wind-rumpled hair. The gleam in his eyes was different, new. "This is a surprise," she managed to get out.

"I thought I was right on time," he countered. "And I'm glad you're coming down for a rest, Sharon. We've got some talking to do."

Chapter Four

"TALKING? What kind of talking?" Sharon asked when she got her breath back.

"The important kind," Tanner said. "Sarah Beth, think you can unhitch yourself from my leg and pick apples for a little while longer?"

"I can unhitch myself," she said, grinning. "But I'm going to go help Mrs. Turner make pies instead. She said she has to make Shane a whole one or he hogs everybody else's. Want me to make you one, too, Daddy?"

"Go right ahead. I'll even eat it." When Sarah Beth had started running toward the house, he turned back to Sharon. "Now, where can we talk?"

"Over here." Sharon led him to the end of the orchard, where all the ripened fruit had been picked. She noticed he was carrying an apple, polishing it idly on his sleeve. "Tanner, did you stop anywhere for lunch?"

55

56 *Kisses Worth Waiting For*

He seemed to think a minute. "Nope. Don't think I did."

"Then start on that apple before you start talking," Sharon said, even though she was dying to know what he had to say. Maybe he was going to try to rehire her again. If so, it was a lost cause, but she'd listen to his speech again.

Tanner worked his way through half the apple in record time. Then he leaned against the tree he was sitting next to and focused his attention on her. She got a shiver in her spine watching him watch her.

"We had some great seminars this weekend. The best one was on personal communications. Like how to stop talking like lawyers and start talking like regular people. I hear it's easier on office staff. And clients. And friends." He took another healthy bite of apple and kept looking at her.

"Anyway, the lecturer was asking everyone to think about the most convoluted conversation they'd had lately. Something where they'd said one thing and meant something completely different. I looked around the room and could see that everyone else was thinking about briefs and wills and some such."

Kisses Worth Waiting For 57

"And what were you thinking about?" Sharon asked.

"All I could think of was a certain bright fall morning and the scent of jasmine in your hair. What kind of shampoo do you use, Sharon? Never mind—that's irrelevant." He laughed, a short bark.

"Now there's a lawyer word for you, just like the lecturer was pointing out. Anyway, I realized I'd left you with the wrong impression that morning." He leaned back more firmly against the tree. "That seminar was Saturday morning, and I couldn't tell you what happened the rest of the day. All I could think about most of the time was getting back here and talking to you."

"You mean kissing me didn't make you feel like a fool?" Sharon blurted out, unable to take the silence any longer.

"Oh, on the contrary, it made me feel more like a fool than I had in years," he told her, finishing his apple. He tossed the core over the fence into some high weeds and gently took her hand. "I didn't feel like a fool because of you, Sharon. I felt like a fool because I couldn't resist the urge to kiss you. But I don't think that came across in our conversation later."

58   *Kisses Worth Waiting For*

"You can say that again," Sharon said, relief flooding her. She knew it showed in the silly grin on her face. "Does this mean it might happen again?"

"Well, I wouldn't go that far," Tanner said, suddenly looking more serious. "Let's just say that I can't dredge up any deep regrets about it, either. You're a very pretty woman, Sharon. Good person on the inside too. But I'm just not ready to take anything anywhere with anybody right now. So don't go blowing that kiss out of proportion, all right?"

"All right." From anyone else she would have called this conversation a total bust. But coming from Tanner, after four years of typing and filing and very little else, it was heaven. "How about we finish up those apples?" She got up and dusted off the seat of her jeans, and he got up beside her.

In the orchard Tanner was good company. He seemed to put a different personality on with his leisure clothes. There was a more relaxed air to him than she'd ever seen. But then, this was the first time she'd ever seen him outside of the office, or a restaurant, or the courthouse, unless you counted twice when she was in the front hall of his

Kisses Worth Waiting For   59

house to deliver things when he had the flu. And then Sarah Beth had taken the papers upstairs.

"Of course you'll stay for dinner," Sharon's mother said when she came out to the orchard to tell them it was ready. It wasn't a question, more of a regal command, and Tanner didn't argue. He pulled up to the table and proceeded to eat more fried chicken than anybody but Shane.

Even Sarah Beth watched him in amazement. "Daddy, that's your fourth piece," she scolded. "You're not going to have room for my pie."

"There's always room for apple pie," he said firmly, pushing away from the table. "Especially if there's coffee to go with it. Have Sharon teach you how to do that. She makes the world's best."

"So that's why you're always downstairs," she teased, getting up to help India clear the plates away.

"You've got it," Tanner said. "You can see the bottom of the cup through Charlotte's. I think she needs more instructions."

"I think you need more tolerance. Can't that woman do anything to suit you?" Sharon asked, heading for the kitchen.

60 *Kisses Worth Waiting For*

"She can type better than you can. Of course, the fact that we installed that fancy new computer with the spell-check and everything might have something to do with that."

"It might." Sharon went into the kitchen.

India followed close behind. "He isn't at all stuffy, Share. Are you sure this is the same guy you've been talking about? I think he's kind of cute."

"I never said he wasn't. And this is the most relaxed I've ever seen him," Sharon said. "I'll make the coffee and you cut the pie."

"Should I bother cutting Shane's or just give him the tin and a fork?"

"Give him a plate and make him be civilized just like everybody else. Just because we're in football season doesn't mean he has to eat like a linebacker every night," Sharon said huffily. "He can get his own second or third piece."

Sarah Beth came into the kitchen and carried her father's pie out to the dining room. The pie was a little lopsided but otherwise looked like a good first effort, and he said so himself. And he ate every bit of it while she watched, entranced.

Kisses Worth Waiting For   61

"See, I told you it would be just fine," Mrs. Turner told her apprentice cook. "Next time we'll make sugar cookies."

Tanner looked at Sharon, a question in his eyes.

"There better be a next time," she told him. "We've all had too good a time for this not to be repeated."

The nodding around the table convinced him. Even Mr. Turner put in a few words. He reached over with a callused hand and rumpled Sarah Beth's hair. "She's quieter than any of the nieces or nephews. Hardly knew she was around the place. We'd love to have her back."

"If you say so. We'll have to work it out then."

The minute her father's words were out of his mouth, Sarah Beth let out the breath she'd been holding in a whoop. "Great! I can hardly wait to come back."

"Well, get next door and pack then, so we can talk about next time," Tanner said. "Right now we have to go home so I can get ready for work tomorrow and you can finish that homework you're about to tell me you don't have."

Sarah Beth went. Sharon and Tanner

62   *Kisses Worth Waiting For*

walked across the yard with her, and they stood on the porch of the small yellow house while she stuffed things into her suitcase upstairs. "She seems to have had a wonderful time. I expect I'll be hearing for a week about what a paragon you are," Tanner said. "Let me do more than just say thank you, all right?"

"You don't need to. I enjoyed this as much as she did," Sharon began, but Tanner, veteran lawyer, had his own argument well in hand.

"I really owe you. Think of what a sitter for the whole weekend would have cost. At least let me take you out to dinner somewhere next week. Can we do that?"

"I guess so. It's India's week to cook, and she won't mind having a night on her own. Name the day and we'll do it."

"Thursday at six," he said without hesitation. "I was so sure of my powers of persuasion, I made the reservations before I left town."

"You're hopeless." Sharon sighed. "But then, after working for you for four years, I knew that already. Can I ask one more question?"

"Sure. Go ahead. After a Sunday dinner

Kisses Worth Waiting For 63

like that you can even have the combination to the safe."

"Okay, Tanner. Then why did you feel like you had to resist? Kissing me, I mean." Sharon's words seemed to be coming out slower than her thoughts as she looked up at him.

He gave it some deep thought. "Because you deserve better, I guess. There's never going to be anything between us, and we both know it. And I didn't want to take advantage of the fact that you're a very pretty young woman."

He gave a deep chuckle, leaning against the porch rail. "I just seem to have noticed that somehow. Sharon, you worked for me for almost four solid years. You were honest, dependable, funny, competent. How come I never noticed you were also beautiful?"

"I haven't the slightest idea, Tanner," Sharon said, a little irritated. "It doesn't seem to do me much good that you've noticed now."

"It may do you plenty of good. I know dozens of eligible young lawyers, bailiffs, police officers. . . ."

"Thanks, but I'll do my own matchmak-

64　　*Kisses Worth Waiting For*

ing. If yours isn't any better than your other mechanical skills. . . ."

"Point taken," he said as Sarah Beth came out on the porch. "See you tomorrow."

Sarah Beth put her bag down and hugged Sharon tightly. "Thanks for everything. I had a good time."

"I'm glad," Sharon told her. "See you tomorrow."

"Another cousin? Come on, Sharon, nobody has that many cousins. Who is this guy?" Tanner lounged in the doorway with his fresh cup of coffee, shirtsleeves rolled up and a wry look on his face.

"I told you, Cousin Sam Mumford. He wants to adopt his wife's kids from her first marriage, and they can't find her ex to sign the papers. I thought you'd want the job."

"Actually, I'm a little strapped for time right now. Why don't you see if Jim can handle it?" he said, looking a bit distant.

"Well, if that's the way you want it . . ." Sharon trailed off, watching Tanner go up the stairs with his coffee cup.

Now what was this about? Maybe Tanner was just being a nice guy, giving his new colleague some business. Charlotte hadn't men-

Kisses Worth Waiting For   65

tioned his caseload being that heavy lately. Sharon shrugged and headed up the stairs herself, stopping at Jim's door.

It looked very official. He'd let her dad come and put his name up on the glass in gold letters. Sharon convinced him it was a free service she provided for all legal clients, not wanting to cost him any of his rapidly dwindling nest egg for the lettering.

Standing there, Sharon got an idea of what this was all about. Tanner was getting sneaky. He knew that this search was going to be long and involved. Jim could handle it fine and had, in fact, done several similar jobs for him when he was working in their office.

Of course he'd need help. The kind of help that Sharon could provide by spending a lot of hours with him. "Oh, Tanner," Sharon muttered under her breath. It was just like him to try and be tricky like this. He never realized she could see right through this kind of scheme.

Well, she could scheme too. She went in and laid out the plan to Jim. He was anxious for the business. "I may need a little help doing some of the searches," he said. He looked excited and serious and ready to

66   *Kisses Worth Waiting For*

start. Sharon liked the way his blue eyes shone and the earnest look on his face. It reminded her of a boy on the first day of school. She thought of Anna Mae and the way her eyes followed Jim every time he came in the front door.

"No problem," she told him. "I've got just the candidate for those long hours in the law library with you." If Tanner wanted matchmaking, he'd get it. Only, the match was going to be of Sharon's choosing.

On Thursday evening Tanner scowled at her when he came to pick her up. "Those two have been spending an awful lot of time together, haven't they?" he asked, watching Jim and Anna Mae go out the front door, laughing.

"I guess so. Somebody had to help him do all his searches for that case you handed over," Sharon said calmly. "Anna Mae has told me she wanted to learn some more about the legal field. She's thinking of going back to school, being a paralegal. I thought this would be a great start."

"So I see. Great start in other directions, too, huh, Sharon?"

"Hmmm?" Sharon slipped her reading glasses into a case and locked them in her

Kisses Worth Waiting For   67

desk drawer. "What kind of start would that be, Tanner?" She stood up and smoothed the skirt of her soft navy dress.

"Well, like I said, they seem to be spending a lot of time together. I mean, whenever I come down for lunch, there's Jim hanging around her desk. And when they leave in the evening, they're always together."

"Only way you could have noticed that is by hanging around this office quite a bit yourself," she said quietly, trying to keep a grin from playing around her face.

"Well, as part owner of this business I've got to make sure it's running smoothly, don't I? Besides, I've told you before that Charlotte makes terrible coffee. I have to come down for sustenance."

"Right. What would you say if I told you that I've made your office coffee for the last three days?"

Tanner actually blushed. "I'd say that I haven't had a cup up there in a week. You caught me, Sharon. If I'm bothering you, I can stay up there."

"No, you don't have to do that." She locked her office door and walked quickly around the outer office to make sure all the machines were turned off and the lights

68 *Kisses Worth Waiting For*

switched off. "But I wish you'd stop coming up with all these excuses and just admit that you like coming down here."

"That's silly. Of course I like coming down here. It's very pleasant. But surely you wouldn't think I'm coming down here just for the company?" He backed into the hall.

"Me? Of course I wouldn't say a thing like that. I never argue with members of the legal profession. It's a lost cause." Sharon shooed Tanner out the front door and locked up after him, listening to him laugh.

The restaurant was lovely. Sharon felt as if she'd walked into the Black Forest, surrounded by brass-band music and cuckoo clocks. The food was good too.

"I'm going to overdose on homemade bread and butter," she groaned, reaching for the bread basket again.

"That makes two of us. This stuff is great." Tanner's hand met hers over the bread basket. It gave her a little shock, meeting the smooth warmth of his fingers. His eyes sparkled, and he squeezed her hand just a little before they separated.

He teased Sharon about the piece of black forest torte for dessert, then ate most of it.

Kisses Worth Waiting For 69

It seemed his fork was sliding over in her direction every time Sharon looked around. Finally she gave up, laughing. "I don't need this." She pushed the plate over to him. "Go ahead. Take it yourself."

He had a look of mock hurt on his face. "I just wanted a taste."

"Yeah, right. A taste of the whipped cream, a taste of the filling, a taste of the cherries, a taste of each layer of cake. Tanner, you're hopeless." But she loved him, anyway, even though she didn't add that out loud. He wasn't ready to hear that yet.

He was ready for a walk. "We've got to stroll off a few of those calories," he told her, holding the door to the restaurant open. They walked down Broadway toward the river, looking in shop windows, strolling at their leisure.

The sky was dark, and lights on barges floating down the river twinkled. Right now the swift water flowing past looked smooth and friendly, and the heavy concrete flood walls looked foolish. But Sharon could remember all too many Octobers where the waters were pushing at the walls themselves.

Life was like that, she mused. Sometimes the current just carried you along and things

70   *Kisses Worth Waiting For*

went smoothly. Like now, with the business taking most of her time and Tanner taking up most of the rest. Then other times the floodgates opened and troubles started lapping around your feet.

Sharon looked down, feeling her heart speed up. The floodgates may not have opened, but the waters were certainly getting swifter. Tanner was holding her hand.

He was strolling along naturally, apparently not even noticing that he had taken her hand and was walking with her. She looked down again, and he answered her unspoken question.

"Yes, Sharon, I know. I tried my best to get you interested in Jim instead. And you saw how well that worked. In fact, I think you did see how well that worked. Another of your infamous cousins came in handy, didn't she?" He turned to her, leaning her up against the floodwall they'd been walking closer and closer to.

"Anyway, it's a beautiful fall night, and there's a big old orange moon out. You're a great person to have dinner with and even better to walk in the moonlight with. And against all my better judgment I'm going to kiss you."

Kisses Worth Waiting For   71

He leaned down, and his lips brushed hers gently. Sharon put a hand softly on his arm, and this time Tanner wasn't frightened away. That alone made her heart beat even faster. He came closer, taking her into his arms, and kissed her slowly and thoroughly.

Sharon wanted to lose herself in this moment for the rest of the night, maybe forever. Maybe she could freeze time for a while, stop the river flowing, and keep Tanner here with his arms wrapped around her. But she knew that her life had to flow forward just like the river, and sweet as this moment was, it wasn't going to last.

Tanner drew away, and after a moment Sharon found her breath. "I think it's time to walk back to the car. I know you need to get home to Sarah Beth, and I have things to do too. Thank you, Tanner. It was a wonderful evening, all of it. And very special."

And I'm not letting it happen again, she told herself. It was too easy to get used to, and that was one thing she just couldn't afford.

Tanner Williams in the moonlight wrapped himself around her heart tighter than he'd wrapped himself around her body. And Sharon knew that was a lost cause. So

72   *Kisses Worth Waiting For*

she walked back to the car with him, both of them quiet, while she thought about a way to end this fascination she had with him.

She thought a very long time, but there were no answers under the light of the big orange moon that followed her all the way home to Scott City. It shone in her bedroom window as she pretended to read, and it shone in even brighter when she turned off the light and tried to go to sleep. No matter how it shone, it still didn't light up any answers. None but the one she had already— to love Tanner whether he wanted her to or not. Deciding that, she slept.

Chapter Five

"**I**T looks nice. Tanner will be pleased," Sharon said, running her hand over the glossy surface of the shelves Paul had just finished installing. The unit looked as if it had always been in the corner of the office, he'd matched it so well to the original woodwork.

"I hope so. Maybe I can get a kind word out of him for a change. That man is awful quiet, isn't he?"

"I guess, around strangers." It was all Sharon could think of to say. With her Tanner wasn't that quiet, but Charlotte complained all the time that she never got more than three words at a stretch out of him.

Of course these days Charlotte complained a lot. She wasn't happy that Sarah Beth still came every day after school. "Isn't almost ten old enough to take herself home and let herself in instead of coming here?" she'd groused at the sink last week. When

73

74   *Kisses Worth Waiting For*

Sharon had opened her mouth to argue, Charlotte hadn't given her a chance, voicing her other complaints fast and furious.

Tanner was too quiet and too picky. And he never drank the coffee she fixed. And he never looked at his appointment calendar, then complained that she never told him what was going on.

Sharon was tempted to tell her she'd be happy to use the resources of Shalimar, Inc., to find her a more suitable position, but that meant she'd probably be stuck interviewing someone else. Heaven knows Tanner would never be pleased with anyone she'd bring up there. It was easier to just give Charlotte a shoulder to cry on—or more likely, complain on—once in a while instead.

Now, however, she had something that would please him. Paul's bookcase was perfect. Looking at it, Sharon couldn't find a single fault that Tanner could bring up. "It looks just perfect," she told Paul again.

"Yeah, well, it isn't even finished yet. I still have one more sanding job to do and the last coat of varnish," Paul said. "And if there are any phone calls for me, have Anna Mae send them up, will you?"

Kisses Worth Waiting For 75

"Sure. What gives? You've looked jumpy for the last couple of days, Paul."

"Well, we finally took Buddy into the doctor's office."

"What's wrong?" Sharon could see from the look on Paul's face it wasn't good news.

"They don't know for sure. Kay's up in St. Louis with him today, at some specialist's. It's either something fairly simple that a round of antibiotics and some therapy will take care of, or some bone disease I've never heard of before. He could be in a cast for six months or need surgery."

"Oh, Paul. I'll make sure Anna Mae puts through any calls right away. Hang in there." She gave his shoulder a squeeze and headed downstairs to try to lose herself in her work.

Noon came and went, and Paul didn't come downstairs. There were plenty of phone calls, but none for him. Sharon thought of him as she unwrapped her solitary sandwich and ate it in the conference room, watching the billowing leaves that were turning on the trees outside.

It truly was autumn out there. There was a bite to the air now all the time, and everything was turning brilliant shades of gold

76   *Kisses Worth Waiting For*

and burnt orange. It looked extremely cheerful, but Sharon was hard-pressed to feel that way. Her thoughts just kept going back upstairs to Paul, working on the shelves and waiting for that infernal phone call.

After she'd crumpled up the paper from her sandwich and gone back to her work, Sharon really had tried to work. But every little noise, telephone ring or anything else, distracted her. Finally she whipped off her reading glasses and shoved them into the case.

"If anybody comes looking for me, I'll be up in Tanner's office with Paul. I can't stand this waiting anymore, and I'll bet he's the same way."

Anna Mae nodded. "He'll tolerate your company better than mine. With any luck you won't be up there long, anyway."

Sharon went up the stairs. Paul looked up when she came into the room. "Well?"

"No phone call. I'm just edgy from sitting down there waiting for one."

Paul nodded, a wry smile on his face for a moment. "Try sitting up here then. It's a real picnic."

For a while Sharon sat quietly and watched him work. She didn't need to talk

Kisses Worth Waiting For   77

to distract him and, being practical, she knew that nothing she could say could truly distract him from the pictures his mind was weaving at that moment, anyway.

"This is driving me nuts," she said, on the verge of exploding half an hour later. At that moment the telephone rang. Paul looked at Sharon. "Yep, it's yours. Charlotte knows not to put Tanner's calls through when he's in court."

Paul picked up the receiver, and Sharon noticed that the brown, work-scarred hand trembled a little bit when he lifted it to his ear. "Hello. Kay?"

There was conversation that held Sharon breathless, watching Paul's face. She tried to imagine Kay, bulky with their second child, trying to lug Buddy around in a cast or sit by his side and entertain him in a children's hospital. Neither picture was pleasant.

Then there was a whoop, and Paul slammed down the receiver. He reached over for Sharon's hand and danced her around the room. "The pills are going to cost fifty-six dollars a bottle, but the little squirt won't have to go into the hospital. No surgery, no cast. We're home free."

Sharon found herself breathless, laughing

78   *Kisses Worth Waiting For*

as they swooped around the room. "Oh, Paul, I'm so glad for you. And Kay."

"And Buddy. Can you imagine that wild man in a cast that long?"

"Never."

They stopped their spin around the floor in front of Tanner's desk. Paul held her shoulders, eyes shining. "Thanks for coming up here. It meant a lot. I was getting close to the edge, waiting up here alone."

"Hey, you're my cousin and my friend," Sharon said. She found herself squeezed by the hug that followed his outburst of laughter.

Neither of them heard the door open, but there stood Tanner in the doorway. "I'll be back in a few minutes," he said in a clipped tone. "I wouldn't want to interrupt anything in my own office." He left, but not before Sharon registered with shock the bleak look on his face as he went.

"Okay, Tanner, what's up?" Sharon walked into the conference room. Tanner stood, staring out the windows, hands jammed into the pockets of his gray-flannel suit.

He turned, and his eyes flashed a little

Kisses Worth Waiting For   79

darker gray than the flannel. "Perhaps I should ask you the same thing. I mean, I wasn't the one having some kind of midday tryst in my office up there."

"Midday tryst? Oh, give me a break!" Sharon exclaimed. "I've told you before, Paul's a cousin. A cousin with a load of medical bills right now, a pregnant wife, and a sick little boy. You show me someone else in more need of a hug, and I'll dole one out." She could feel the color rising in her face while she spoke. She was somewhere between simmer and boil right now, and Tanner was trying his best to turn up the heat.

"You always have a perfect excuse, don't you, Sharon?" Tanner sounded tired, and his shoulders were drooping. "There are cousins for everything, and they all happen to turn up at the proper times. If we need anything done around here, lo and behold, a cousin shows up to do it. And now I come in from a rotten morning in court, my secretary's gone, the phone's ringing off the hook, and all I want is my own office. Except there's my ex-office manager in it, embracing a handsome guy. And wouldn't you know it, he's her cousin. Only the forty-seventh one I've encountered this month."

80   *Kisses Worth Waiting For*

"You really don't believe me, do you?" Sharon's voice came out even flintier than Tanner's accusing tone. "Well, then, you and I are taking a walk upstairs. Now."

Paul, packing up the last of his supplies and tools, lost his grin when he saw the look on Sharon's face. "Can I do something for you?" He stood up and brushed his hands off on his overalls.

"Yeah. Pull out your wallet for me, will you, Paul?"

Paul looked puzzled, but he did it. He opened the worn brown-leather wallet and handed it to Sharon. "If something's missing around here, you can have anything you want, wallet and all. I'm innocent."

Sharon felt a flush of new anger. "Nothing like that. I just wanted to show Tanner your driver's license. And the lovely picture of you and Kay and Buddy taken last Christmas that's next to it."

She handed it all to Tanner, watching the ice in his eyes melt as he looked at it. "Paul Turner."

"That's the name on the business card, if you'd bothered to look, mister. It's been on your desk for a week. Now if you want to

Kisses Worth Waiting For   81

inspect these shelves, I have someplace to go."

Sharon slipped out the door, leaving Tanner to deal with her cousin. She knew he'd have a word or two to say to Tanner. Paul had always been as protective of her as he'd been of India or his own little sister. And the mere hint that someone hadn't believed Sharon wasn't going to set well with him, she could tell.

In a few minutes Paul stuck his head into the office. "Man upstairs says you cut the checks. I'll send you a bill once I get home and whirl Buddy around a few times, okay?"

"Fine," Sharon said, trying to raise some enthusiasm. "I'm glad for you, Paul. And the check will be in the mail as soon as I get the bill. Better yet, what do you say that India and I have you three over to dinner one night next week?"

"Only if you cook. I'm not going for another nut-loaf casserole. Ever."

"Don't worry," Sharon said, managing a laugh. "Now she's into salads and vegetable soup. But I'll cook, anyway. I'll call Kay and set it up, all right?"

"Sounds good. And, Sharon?"

"Yes?"

82 *Kisses Worth Waiting For*

"I think he'd be okay if he gave himself a chance. That man really doesn't want anybody else messing with you, does he?"

Sharon thought of Tanner's image in the conference-room windows earlier. "I don't think so. Trouble is, he doesn't want to mess with me, either."

"Maybe. Maybe not," Paul said, a small smile starting. "I wouldn't bet big money on that."

"Oh, go find your family, Paul," Anna Mae chided, sticking her head in the office, pushing her brother gently out toward the front door. "If you get her all upset, I'll have to deal with her all afternoon. Do not, I repeat, do not start Sharon thinking any more about Tanner. I've just about got her cured."

They were both laughing as they left Sharon to try to untangle the mess she'd left earlier on her desk. Of course, there was an even bigger mess to untangle upstairs, but she wanted no part of that.

Was Tanner really that jealous and that untrusting? And what was there to be jealous of in the first place, if indeed he was? It made Sharon's temples throb just thinking of all the possibilities. She massaged them as she leaned back in her chair. Just as she got

Kisses Worth Waiting For 83

ready to open her eyes and go back to work, there was a slam of the front door. Hurricane Sarah Beth had found land.

"So no problem. If you have a headache, I can stay upstairs for a change," Sarah Beth said. "Do you want me to get you an aspirin or something? Charlotte keeps plenty of headache stuff upstairs."

"No, thanks, sweetie. And I'd tiptoe around up there too. Last time I went up, there were some storm warnings."

"Oh, great. You have a headache, and Daddy's in one of his moods. Think he'll let me go get his house key and let myself in for a change? Ginger lent me this great movie, and it's in my backpack."

"Why don't you go up and see? Tell him I'll even drive you home if he doesn't want you walking."

"You sure you want to, with your headache and all?"

"Fresh air will do me good," Sharon assured her. "Now scoot."

In a few minutes Sarah Beth was back. She hadn't thundered down the stairs for once. "Daddy said I could go home. And he said it would be nice if you'd give me a ride. Do you still want to?"

84   *Kisses Worth Waiting For*

"For you? Anytime." Sharon grabbed her purse, told Anna Mae where she was going, and took off. The crisp air felt good rushing by the car window. It really did have an effect on her headache. Maybe she just had cobwebs in her head from trying to untangle her problems inside on a glorious day like this.

When she pulled up in front of the house, Sarah Beth insisted that she come in.

"Just for a minute," Sharon relented. "I really have to get back to work."

"What a drag!" Sarah Beth said, smiling. "You were right. Daddy was in a growly mood up there. Honestly, I don't see how Mrs. Mackelroy stands him, do you?"

Sharon let that question hang in the air. She wasn't about to try to answer it today. "You want any help fixing a snack or anything before I leave, Sarah Beth?"

"Come on, Sharon." Sarah Beth stood in the front hallway, hands on the hips of her faded jeans. "I fix half the suppers around here. I think I can handle cookies and milk."

"Okay, I forgot," Sharon said, holding up her hands in defense. She followed Sarah Beth down the hall to the kitchen. The rooms in between were clean but sounded

Kisses Worth Waiting For　85

very empty. The kitchen was, without doubt, where Tanner and Sarah Beth lived together.

It was cluttered, and there was an art gallery and a myriad of notices, from grade-school menus to hastily scrawled phone numbers, on the refrigerator. A bulletin board held even more paraphernalia. Clear canisters held cookies, snacks, rice, and dry beans all stacked in neat rows on the countertops. There were cheerful curtains and plenty of light. Sharon could see the two of them sitting at the big wooden table in the morning, having breakfast before they went off to start their day.

"This is a nice room," she told Sarah Beth, who had her head in the refrigerator, looking for the milk.

Her eyes were wide when she backed out. "You mean you've never been in here before? Sharon, I kind of think of you as part of the family. Hasn't Daddy ever had you over before?"

"Well, I've brought stuff over when he's been sick before, but I've never made it farther than the front hallway."

Sarah Beth shook her head and grabbed Sharon's hand. "Come on, you're getting the tour." Before Sharon could protest, she was

86 *Kisses Worth Waiting For*

pulling her up the stairs to show her the rest of the house.

Sarah Beth's room didn't hold many surprises. It was full of stuffed animals, posters, and a personal computer. "Sometimes Dad takes it into his room and uses it when I let him. But mostly it's mine," Sarah Beth explained. The walls were a neutral beige, and there were no ruffles on the bedspread, Sharon noticed. Like Sarah Beth herself, it wasn't terribly feminine except in the detail.

Just as Sarah Beth wore little bits of jewelry along with the vivid shirts and jeans she favored, her room had hints of a girl growing up. There was a tiny lace pillow on the bed, and from somewhere came the scent of a floral cologne. On the bureau next to the markers and scattered change was a bottle of lilac nail polish. Sharon could see her in her mind's eye, sitting near the lamp at night, tongue out in concentration as she used it.

Once again she ached to put her arms around those narrow shoulders and do all kinds of "girl stuff" with her, as Sarah Beth would call it. But she knew that just like her father, Sarah Beth would shy away from anything that open in the way of declarations of affection. So Sharon held her peace

Kisses Worth Waiting For   87

and followed Sarah Beth through the rest of the upstairs.

There was a guest room, with a sewing machine in a cabinet that served as an end table. "I don't think it's been opened since Grandma came two years ago and did a whole bunch of mending and made my new curtains," Sarah Beth said, grinning. "Daddy has this secret way of getting buttons to hold with some thread and a safety pin until he takes things to the cleaners. He says it's more efficient that way."

"I'll bet." Sewing on buttons would come under the heading of mechanics, Sharon thought. And that was not Tanner's arena at home or at work.

In front of the other closed door on that floor, Sharon balked. "You don't need to show me that room, Sarah Beth."

"Don't worry, he makes his bed," she said, flinging the door open. Inside was a quiet blue-and-white room, very tailored and extremely neat. Tanner did, in fact, make his bed. There wasn't much else in the room that could have been out of place.

There were no pictures and only a single dresser with a mirror. One chair, with a silk tie draped over the back and a pair of folded corduroys on the seat, completed the total furnishings of the room.

"Downstairs he's got his study. It's a pit. Want to see?"

"Not today. I've got to get back before Anna Mae thinks I'm being held for ransom," Sharon said. "You go ahead with your snack, and I'll see you Monday, okay?"

"Fine. Hope your headache gets better."

"It's already almost gone," Sharon told her, watching her close the door behind her, listening for the snick of the lock. If Tanner asked, she wanted to make sure she could report that everything was safe and sound.

Not that she wanted to see Tanner again today. The thought of his telling her what he thought of her still remained with her. Sharon knew she wasn't going to be able to shake it for quite a while.

So maybe she did have a lot of cousins, and maybe plenty of them trooped through the offices. But all of it was legitimate business, and there was no sense in not giving it to family first.

And maybe she was more outgoing than Tanner had ever thought her to be. Just because he'd seen her hugging Paul today was

Kisses Worth Waiting For   89

no cause for getting upset. It was just like Tanner to misconstrue everything.

Like that time last month that Ed had come by to adjust the thermostat and needed help with the one on the second floor. He'd only been steadying the chair behind her, but Tanner had sure given them an odd look. Almost as odd a look as he'd given Cousin Sid Bradley this summer when Sharon had been chasing him with the hose outside after he'd dumped that handful of ice down the back of her shirt when she was helping plant the last of the shrubs around the front door.

Sharon got the giggles. All right, she had to admit it. She had a big, rambunctious family. And for a sedate only child, with the mind of a picky lawyer, maybe there was a lot going on. She'd have to give Tanner another chance, if he'd give her one. Now if only there was a way to make him understand.

She had a smile on her face when she came into the front hall, and under her breath she was even humming. Tanner was coming down the stairs and did his best to look serious and contrite.

"Sharon, if I got out of line up there,

90   *Kisses Worth Waiting For*

please forgive me," he said, starting some long apology.

"Already done," she replied, tucking one of the pale purple mums she'd picked on the front walk into his buttonhole. "Now just be good and leave me alone for the rest of the afternoon, okay? I've got six client statements and four new proposals to get on Anna Mae's desk before I leave."

"Fine," he said, sounding dazed. "Aren't you going to yell at me or anything?"

"Wouldn't do any good," she answered simply as she walked into her office. "So I'm not going to waste my breath with it anymore. Have a nice weekend, Tanner. I know I intend to. I'm going out with a whole bunch of my cousins on a hayride."

That, she knew, would keep him from opening her door. Sharon slid on her reading glasses and turned on the computer. Anna Mae was going to have a full desk tonight. And with any luck Tanner Williams would have plenty to think about. It was the first time Sharon could remember that she had kept her opinion to herself after a discussion with him. That alone should keep him thinking about her until Monday.

She pushed her glasses higher on the

Kisses Worth Waiting For   91

bridge of her nose and smiled. The thought of Tanner thinking about her did that. The screen in front of her hummed to life. "Time's a-wasting," she said out loud, calling up the first client statement she needed to revise. In the pale-green glow of the screen she could see another glint—the glint of warm gray eyes, as thoughts of Tanner kept her progress on her work very, very slow.

Chapter Six

SHARON found it hard to concentrate Saturday morning when her father came to put in the last of the equipment in the new file room. It was going to be just the way she'd envisioned it, efficient and workable, with a computer station in the room as well as the big lateral files that Dad and his assistant were putting in.

"I really ought to be doing something for you because of this. You've done too much for free," Sharon told her father. She knew what his answer would be, knowing as she did where her stubborn behavior was inherited from.

"Don't bother. I built shelves for Shane last week for his record collection. And India's after me to build in a big storage unit for her bedroom. I might as well 'cause she's probably never going to move out and get married." His bright-blue eyes were rolling skyward. "I mean, honestly, she can't cook, she doesn't sew. . . ."

"Oh, join the modern world, Dad," Sharon said, only half teasing. "India will get married if and when she wants to, and chances are whoever marries her won't care whether she can do either of those things."

"I hope not," her father said with a note of finality. "Because if he does care, he'll be awful disappointed."

Sharon shook her head. There was no use arguing with her father. If she did, she'd get to hear his lecture on how he'd given up on ever being the father of the bride. And, to tell the truth, she would have to agree with him today, at least in her case.

She wasn't getting anywhere with Tanner. His actions were odd, to say the least. How could anyone that uninterested be that jealous at the same time? Sharon decided to use the time to get caught up on her reports and headed for her desk.

She'd been there about an hour when there was a knock on the frame of the open door behind her. "It's open for a reason," Sharon said absently as she jotted some notes on the margin of a report.

"Always the trusting soul. I could be an

Kisses Worth Waiting For   95

ax murderer," Tanner muttered, standing in front of her. He was in jeans and a sweater, and Sharon noticed that there was a small, bright-orange leaf stuck in his hair. It was so tempting to stand up and pluck it out of its nest among the chestnut waves.

Sarcasm won out instead. After all, she had an image to maintain and pride to protect. "So what's the difference between you and an ax murderer, anyway, Tanner? Both of you would keep me from getting done this morning."

"If I'm in the way. . . ."

"No more so than usual," she said, leaning her elbows on the desk. "So what is it this time? Paper stuck in the copier? Can't decipher Charlotte's filing system?"

"Coming to offer a heartfelt apology," he broke in, making her lean back in surprise.

"You did that yesterday," she said. "No need for a repeat performance."

"Yes, there is. I made an utter fool of myself yesterday, and I still feel bad about it." He pulled up a chair and sat next to the desk. "I had to go home and admit to myself that I'm jealous. And that made me admit something even less easy."

"Which was?" Sharon suddenly felt her

tongue cleave to the roof of her mouth in dry anticipation.

"That I think I'm in love with you, Sharon." He looked dazed. "I don't want to be. It really isn't something I would have planned."

"Oh, thank you so very much," she said, starting to rise.

He put a hand on her shoulder. "Now, don't get all steamed up at me, Sharon. That's not the way I mean this at all. It's just that I hadn't planned on falling in love with anybody. I wasn't looking for any kind of relationship. Or at least I didn't think I was. But then last night, thinking hard, I came home. And the smell of your perfume was in the kitchen and the hall and everywhere. And I didn't mind a bit."

"Didn't you?"

Tanner's smile was shy and slow and warmed Sharon to the core. "Not a bit. Now, I can't make any promises about anything. After all—"

"I know—this wasn't in the game plan. Don't rub it in, Tanner."

"I won't. I couldn't." He paused for a moment, looking at her and seeming to see her

Kisses Worth Waiting For   97

in a different light than he ever had before. "Is your hair really as soft as it looks?"

Sharon felt the laughter she'd been keeping back, part panic and part unbelievable happiness, beginning to bubble out of her. "I don't know. But I do know it doesn't have any leaves in it."

Tanner put a hand to his head. "And mine does. Oh, that sure ups my image as a suave man about town, doesn't it? Sarah Beth was helping me rake before she went over to Ginger's."

"That's all right. It's a nice change. I mean, you're always so formal and put together around here. It would do you good to be different for a change."

"Oh? How different do you want me to be?" He reached out and ran his hands up her arms, making her shiver on the inside. His voice got heavy, huskier. "I suspect I could be pretty different if you gave me a chance."

They were both half risen out of their chairs, and Tanner was leaning in to kiss her when there was a cough at the doorway. "This fella giving you any trouble, Rose?" Her father's silhouette seemed even bulkier than usual.

98   *Kisses Worth Waiting For*

Tanner's hands dropped off her arms as if he'd been stung, and he stood up quickly.

"No, not at all," Sharon said, trying to keep her voice level. "We were just discussing some . . . personal business."

"I'll say. Those files are against the wall now. Want to come see if the spacing is right?"

"Yes." Sharon stood and looked at Tanner. "Do you want lunch?"

"With you? Definitely. What time?"

"I'll come up when I'm ready. And, Tanner?"

"Yes?"

"Stop looking like a high-schooler. Dad's gruff and protective, but he wouldn't bite. Ever." Sharon gave him a smile as she left the room.

Lunch. Sharon had to remind herself to concentrate on keeping the huge, drippy sandwich from their favorite barbecue place from falling into her lap. It wasn't easy while trying to talk to Tanner today. He was so interested, and interesting, that it made eating secondary.

"He called you Rose."

Sharon grimaced. "He still does. Nobody

Kisses Worth Waiting For   99

else ever does, not even Shane, if he knows what's good for him. But Dad I can't stop."

"So it's really your name?"

"It is. But don't you dare. Ever."

"Why'd you change it?"

She leaned her elbows on the table and looked at Tanner, hard. "You've been in my mom's house now. What's the dominating characteristic?"

He leaned back in his chair, looking as if he were trying to reconstruct the place in his memory. "Besides the books?"

"No, that's it. We asked her to count how many there were, just in the dining room one time. When she got to four hundred, she gave up, and so did we. And, Tanner, that's just the dining room."

He chuckled. "So saying she's a literary buff would be easy. What does that have to do with your being named Rose?"

"Not just Rose. Rose Sharon. As in Rose-of-Sharon, as in Steinbeck's *Grapes of Wrath.* She threatened to actually name me Rose-of-Sharon, but my father drew the line."

"Good man." Tanner went to work on his second sandwich. Where he put them was a mystery to Sharon.

She nodded. "She tended to name us all

100   *Kisses Worth Waiting For*

from her favorite characters in her books. My sister India—from *Gone With the Wind*—is forever thankful she's female. Ashley would have been hard to deal with in high school, I suspect."

"I think Shane got the best of the deal."

"Perhaps. None of us actually suffered from it. I mean, it could have been a lot worse. The Mumfords all tend to go in for naming trends. I have cousins Ed, Fred, and Ted. And then there's Jolene, Jordan, Joellyn, and Joel."

"Not to mention Matthew, Mark, Luke, and Joann," Tanner said with a wicked grin.

"How did you know?" she asked.

He nearly dropped his sandwich. "I was kidding."

"I wasn't." She split into a wide grin. "Now you can see why I'm happy with plain old Sharon. And besides, you have little room to tease. Garth Tanner?"

"Yeah, well, they're family names," he said defensively. "My grandmother was big on that, and she insisted. It could have been worse for me too. Her brother was named Kermit."

"Obviously your wife chose Sarah Beth's name all by herself."

Kisses Worth Waiting For 101

"Correct," Tanner said, smiling. "My grandmother was holding out for Naomi or some such, but Tory was adamant. She usually was about most things." He looked down at his plate, suddenly more somber.

"You still miss her?" It was half statement, half question, and Sharon longed to put her hand on top of his while she asked.

"I miss the idea of her, I guess. It's been long enough now that the memories are getting fuzzy around the edges. I think about things and wonder how they would have turned out. I can't really connect the image of the young woman Tory was with what she'd be like now, given the chance."

"Sarah Beth told me it was cancer."

He nodded. "Fairly quick but hardly painless. It was so ironic. After all those years of student housing, tiny little apartments with a tricycle out front, always living on peanut butter and macaroni and cheese, we'd finally made it. We had the house, my student-loan balance was coming down nicely. I mean, we were even talking about buying a new car." He looked up at Sharon, his eyes deep-gray pools stirred with pain. "Do you know I never bought her an anniversary gift that cost more than a week's gro-

102   *Kisses Worth Waiting For*

ceries? Heck, half the time I even forgot the anniversary."

"I'm sorry," Sharon said. She didn't know how to respond to the pain and the hint of anger in his voice.

"Yeah, well, no use regretting it now. But at least you can figure out why I say falling in love isn't in the game plan. I wouldn't wish the life Tory had with me on a dog."

Sharon sat back in her chair, watching Tanner attack the rest of his last sandwich. For once she had absolutely no comeback. She suspected that Tory would have had a vastly different picture of their life together, but there was no way she could have gotten Tanner to see that.

She noticed the pattern of the wood of the table in front of her. It was a rich, whorling oak. As she ran her fingers over it, she had the urge to laugh. Not a happy laugh, but one of deep irony. If anyone had told her earlier today that Tanner would tell her he loved her and that she would be devastated by it, she would have called them a fool. But this statement coming so quick on the heels of the other one was worse than anything she could have imagined.

So Tanner loved her. And he wouldn't

Kisses Worth Waiting For 103

marry again for anything because of regrets he had about a life he'd led with a woman who could no longer describe it. Sharon sat and watched Tanner put away a piece of apple pie with ice cream on top and was totally truthful when she told him she didn't even want a spoonful of the ice cream.

"Tell me again how I let you talk me into this," Sharon said, watching Tanner slip on a sweater over his shirt.

"It's simple. I said I'd never been on a hayride and that Sarah Beth had never been on a hayride, and you said we should go on one. And then—"

"You promptly invited yourself on this one," Sharon said crisply. It was hard to be angry at Tanner, looking as good as he did. Sarah Beth was bouncy with excitement. She and Missy had found each other and were taking turns talking Missy's father into letting them sit on the seat of the tractor that was going to pull the hay wagon.

Sharon had made all the introductions, and Tanner's eyes had widened with all the cousins, but he'd been good for a change. Of course, Paul and Kay were there, and Paul had given him a look that had dared him to

104 *Kisses Worth Waiting For*

make even one snide remark. Tanner seemed to have plenty of respect for Paul, especially watching the way he got Kay settled on the wagon as if she were made of cut glass.

Once the hayride started, Sarah Beth was up front with the squealing children throwing handfuls of hay at each other. Tanner watched them, a smile on his face. "That is juvenile behavior and will be tolerated only in the front of the wagon, Tanner," Sharon warned him, watching the glint in his eyes. "The adults sit back here and like it that way. Got it?"

"Got it. But it does take the fun out of things, Ro . . . Sharon." He raised both hands, palms toward her as she grabbed a double handful of hay. "It won't happen again, I promise. It's just that I happen to like Rose. It's a nice, old-fashioned name, even if it doesn't suit you as well."

Sharon put the hay down and gave him what she hoped was a serious look. "You better remember that promise, Tanner. I don't need this whole crew teasing me. They have long memories and quirky senses of humor."

"I'll remember," he said with a straight

Kisses Worth Waiting For   105

face. He moved over, encouraged by the rocking of the wagon to settle in next to her.

It felt wonderful to have him there, even though a small voice was telling Sharon not to enjoy it too much.

That was almost impossible. Tanner's warm, long legs in blue jeans matched hers stretched out on the fragrant, prickly hay. His cologne blended with the fall night, and he was so close. As the darkness grew around them on the country path, there was less talk from the cousins around them. Even the children in the front of the wagon had stopped shrieking.

Tanner leaned over and nuzzled her neck under her ear. Sharon made a sound that wasn't words, exactly, just pleasure. He hadn't shaved that morning and left a little trail of prickly kisses up to her ear.

She turned to meet his kiss, wondering if the jump that her heart had made the first time he'd kissed her had been just a one-time experience. In a moment she discovered it hadn't been. It was so easy to relax here, feeling his arm curl around her, enjoying the texture of his wavy hair twined in her fingers.

All too soon the tractor stopped and Tanner drew back. Everyone was sliding off the

106   *Kisses Worth Waiting For*

hay wagon, one cousin starting a bonfire, another getting out a picnic basket, someone asking Paul if he'd brought his guitar.

"Do you think I'd have let him get on the wagon without it?" Kay asked. "I knew everyone would want him to play something."

The fire blazed as they sat around in a circle, watching the sparks fly up in the crisp fall air. Sarah Beth sat with a stick in the fire, roasting marshmallows. "Daddy, do you really like yours burned?"

"Truly," he said, blowing out the flames on the end of her stick.

"Ugh. Doesn't it make the s'more taste like charcoal?" Sarah Beth shuddered.

"Not at all." He took a bite to prove his point, then offered it to Sharon.

She shook her head. "This is one time I agree with Sarah Beth. Just make mine lightly toasted." She hugged the girl, who smiled and put two marshmallows back over the fire.

Sharon found herself leaning against Tanner's knees, listening to Paul sing. In the background someone else joined in, until they were all singing the words to an old song everyone seemed to know. She was surprised to find that Tanner had a good singing

Kisses Worth Waiting For   107

voice. She'd heard him speak plenty of times, including formal presentations in court and in front of the bar group in town, but singing was new.

"You can sing," he said, seemingly as surprised as she, putting an arm around her.

"I can crochet, too, but you'd never know it."

"There's plenty about you that's surprising me, Sharon. And I'm enjoying every minute of it," he said with a sincerity that made her heart ache.

Sharon forced the ache far from her and leaned into the shoulder he offered her. For tonight she was going to join Tanner in his enjoyment without worrying about tomorrow.

Sarah Beth was beginning to droop by the time the wagon made the circle back to where they all had parked their cars. As the cousins were making their good-byes, Sharon made sure that all of Sarah Beth's and Tanner's things were getting stowed in their car.

"The hayride was nice," Sarah Beth said sleepily as she stretched out on the backseat of the car. "I had a really good time. Thanks, Sharon."

108   *Kisses Worth Waiting For*

"Anytime. You're fun to have around," she told her, meaning it.

"Do you like roller coasters?"

"Love them."

"Daddy says they're monster machines from—"

"Another planet," Tanner ended her sentence.

"That's not where you usually say they're from, Daddy," Sarah Beth chided. "Anyway, since my birthday's on Tuesday, we're not doing anything then, but my official birthday for all the fun stuff is going to be next Saturday."

"That's nice," Sharon said.

Sarah Beth yawned, a large, slow yawn that made Sharon want to join her. "Anyway, we're going to Six Flags, and I told Daddy if we took along a friend, he wouldn't have to go on the Screaming Eagle with me. Want to come?"

Sharon looked at Tanner, who nodded. "I kind of expected another nine-year-old, but you'd be more fun."

"Then I'll be happy to come. Just tell me what time, and I'll be there with bells on."

"Great," Sarah Beth said around another yawn.

Kisses Worth Waiting For   109

"I've got to go home and put this child to bed," Tanner said. He pulled Sharon close to him. "The hayride was fun. Let's do it again sometime."

"We will," Sharon promised.

He squeezed her, a swift, warm hug, and smiled. "Good. I look forward to any chance to see you in blue jeans. It's a heartwarming experience, especially after all those serious little suits and dresses with bows. Sleep tight."

He looked down into the car. Sarah Beth was leaning over, eyes closed, breathing even. "Guess we won't disturb her," he said softly. He kissed Sharon softly, a lingering, sweet kiss that she returned, settling deeper and deeper in his embrace.

"This could be habit-forming," he told her. "I guess I'd better watch myself."

"After a kiss like that, you'd better watch me, Tanner," Sharon said, almost breathless.

He ran a finger down the bridge of her nose. "That's okay. Watching you is definitely more fun. See you Monday."

He slid into the car and started the engine, leaving Sharon smiling under the harvest moon.

In the morning India remarked on Shar-

110 *Kisses Worth Waiting For*

on's cheerfulness. "Must have been some hayride. I'm sorry I worked at the store instead."

"It was a great hayride. I can't think of a paycheck I've ever gotten that would have convinced me to miss it," Sharon told her.

"Mmmm. More must have heated up than the bonfire. Wait till I tell Shane," India said with a grin.

Sharon was in such a good mood she let the remark go. Heading for the shower, she shook her head. When she didn't even feel like worrying about India's teasing, it must really be love. She hummed a tune on her way to the shower, conscious of the smell of woodsmoke still in her hair.

Chapter Seven

SHARON looked over the conference room one last time. It looked as good as she wanted it to. Pink and lilac crepe-paper streamers twisted down from the ceiling, and a frosted cake sat in the middle of the table, with ten candles ringed around the edges. Sarah Beth would enjoy it after a long day at the amusement park.

She went out into the parking lot to wait for Tanner and Sarah Beth. In a few minutes they drove up, the child nearly hanging out the car window with excitement. "Good— you're ready," she said. "Daddy nearly skinned me this morning 'cause I said I had to wash my hair first, and he said women are always late for everything, and I bet him a quarter you'd be here waiting for us. Pay up," she told him smugly, putting out a hand to her father.

"I should have known you'd let me down," Tanner said teasingly to Sharon.

112   *Kisses Worth Waiting For*

"You're almost never late for anything. Count on you to be dependable."

"I'll make it a point to be late the next time we do something if it's that important," she promised, sliding into the car.

She was really enjoying Tanner in sports clothes. He tended toward plaid shirts in bright reds and blues, and trim-fitting jeans or cords. Granted, he did more for a suit than anyone Sharon had ever met, but something told her this was the real Tanner Williams.

"I hope you wore comfortable shoes," he said. "Keeping up with Sarah Beth at someplace like this is a challenge." He picked up a box off the front seat and handed it back to his daughter.

"In here are markers, a new book, countless sheets of computer paper, and a map. I do not expect to hear 'How long is it now?' or, 'When do we get there?' anytime in the next ninety minutes. Got that?"

"Got it," Sarah Beth said, taking the box. "Honestly, Daddy, you're treating me like a little kid. But I'll take the markers, anyway. Mine are about worn-out."

"This is my favorite time of year for a

Kisses Worth Waiting For   113

drive north," Sharon said a little later. "I love all the colors."

Tanner nodded. "And they're especially good this year. More red than usual, I think. Yes, it's a very special fall." Behind them in the backseat Sarah Beth giggled a little, and Sharon wondered what was going on.

After an hour Tanner stretched broadly and draped his right arm over the seat. "Need to work the kinks out of the muscles," he said with a grin, squeezing her shoulder. Sharon took his hand and massaged the fingers, the wrist, and the forearm, enjoying the smooth texture of his hand, the pale-brown hairs glinting in the sunshine below his rolled-up sleeve. Then she guided his hand gently back to the steering wheel.

"Got to watch that road," she told him. It made Sharon smile to watch the warm grin that spread across his face.

"Caught, huh? Well, maybe later." He whistled along with the radio as he drove.

The sun was warm through the windshield, and Sharon felt herself getting drowsy. She opened her purse and fished around for her sunglasses. "I have this failing you've never found out about."

114 *Kisses Worth Waiting For*

"Oh, no. You snore," Tanner said, still looking ahead to the highway.

"Tanner!" Sharon tapped him playfully with the sunglasses case. "I do no such thing. But I do sleep in cars, if I'm not driving."

"So I'll wake you up when we get there." He shrugged. "Or maybe not. I'd save a lot of money if I didn't have to pay another adult admission."

She leaned back on the seat, determined to ignore the teasing. Tanner had teased her, one way or another, since they'd gotten comfortable working together years ago. Lately the teasing had taken a whole new tone, warmer and more intimate somehow.

That didn't disturb Sharon. And it certainly didn't bother her enough to keep her awake long. One moment the sycamores and oaks were blazing past, and the next there was the crunch of the car stopping on a parking lot. Sharon sat up slowly. Just a few hundred yards away the park rose up, with the curve of the roller-coaster tracks rising high above everything else.

"It's catching," Tanner said, motioning to the backseat, where Sarah Beth was slumped over against the door. "And she really does

Kisses Worth Waiting For   115

snore, even if she gets a little upset if I tell anyone about it."

"I won't let on that I know," Sharon promised, reaching back to take Sarah Beth by the shoulder and wake her up. For a moment she just sat and watched her sleep. Awake, she could profess to be a grown-up person. Asleep, she still looked like a child, a lock of hair falling softly on her face. Sharon almost hated to wake her.

But Sarah Beth had waited for days to have fun at the amusement park, and Sharon knew she wouldn't want to miss a minute of it. She shook her shoulder, softly calling her name.

Sarah Beth opened her eyes and smiled slowly. "Great. We're here. Which coaster do you want to do first, Sharon?"

"I guess the Screaming Eagle, at least the first time."

"First time? You mean you crazy people are going to ride that thing more than once?" Tanner, walking with them toward the entrance, looked shocked.

"Sure," they both chorused.

"I should have brought my law journals, after all," he said. "It's going to be a long day."

116   *Kisses Worth Waiting For*

There were plenty of rides Tanner did go on with them. It was just the things that defied the force of gravity he wasn't so wild about. Most of the other attractions he cheerfully stood in line for and rode on. More than once he took advantage of the closeness between seats to slip an arm around Sharon. She knew she would always remember this day as the feel of cool fall breezes and the smell of leaves and Tanner's cologne.

They saw a show at the dolphin pool, sitting a few rows back. "I am not getting splashed by those animals," Tanner said firmly. Sarah Beth grinned, and Sharon thought she was plotting something.

"I'm hungry," Sarah Beth finally announced. "I'm sure it's past lunchtime."

"Twelve on the nose," Tanner informed her.

"Well, for me, that's past lunchtime. We've got the first shift in the cafeteria. On a weekday I'd be done by now."

"No wonder you're always starved when you come over," Sharon said.

They found the nearest restaurant and inhaled hot dogs with Sarah Beth. They tasted good, slathered with mustard. Sharon gig-

Kisses Worth Waiting For   117

gled when Tanner took a napkin, balled it up, and batted at her nose.

"Would you like to explain how you got mustard there?" he asked.

"Haven't a clue, but thanks for getting it off," Sharon replied.

It was uncanny. She felt almost like a family with the two of them, bouncing through the amusement park. After lunch Tanner declared a two-hour moratorium on roller coasters and thrill rides. He consented to ride the skyway across the park, holding on to both of their hands and looking slightly ill at ease. Sharon could tell that this time he wasn't holding on just to be friendly.

It was hard for her not to smile. So the man who fearlessly took on the toughest legal cases in three counties actually had some fears. To Sharon it made him even more attractive. She and Sarah Beth kept their promise not to rock the car, much to his gratitude.

Tanner talked them into watching a music show at the amphitheater. At first Sarah Beth balked at listening to country music, but even she enjoyed the handsome blond singer and his raucous band. Sharon did, too, especially the ballads. She noticed Tanner

118   *Kisses Worth Waiting For*

tapping his foot to the music. He looked so relaxed in the sunshine and didn't seem to notice he'd put an arm around her again. Sharon let it stay there.

"All right, if you want to ride another one of those things, go ahead," Tanner said after the concert. "I can see how you're eyeing the loop on that one . . . what's it called? . . . the Ninja. Where do they come up with the names for these things, anyway? I'll be right here on this bench. Happy landings."

He waved them off, and when they came back, Sharon had to admit that for once even she was breathless.

"Let's find something just a little calmer, okay?" she asked Sarah Beth.

Her eyes brightened and she grinned. "I know—let's do the log flume. I haven't ridden that all day. You'll go with us on that, won't you, Daddy? I mean, everybody goes on that."

"I guess so. It's pretty tame," Tanner said.

The line wasn't too long, and soon they found themselves on the ride. Sarah Beth insisted on taking the front of the log-shaped car, leaving Sharon and Tanner alone in the middle seat. Tanner was comfortable for the

Kisses Worth Waiting For   119

first part of the ride. Then, near the end, he looked pointedly at his daughter's back.

"You conveniently forgot to remind me about the drop-off at the end, didn't you, Peanut? I'll get you for this sometime this week."

Sharon took his hand firmly. "It's not that bad. And it's real fast, anyway, Tanner," she said, trying to tease him out of his discomfort.

As the ride clattered up to the top of the slide down, Sarah Beth looked over her shoulder.

"Could you lean forward with me, Sharon? That way we'll go even faster and it will be over quicker."

"Sweet child," Tanner muttered between clenched teeth just before the drop-off.

At the bottom of the slide was a large pool, and Sharon realized all too late what her and Sarah Beth's leaning forward was going to do. The wash from the splash of the car sliding into the pool arced into their faces. Mostly into Tanner's face, to be accurate.

He pulled out his handkerchief while Sarah Beth laughed so hard she could hardly get off the ride. "Got you, got you, got you," she caroled.

120   *Kisses Worth Waiting For*

"Be thankful it's a warm day. Be very thankful it's a warm day." Outside the ride he sat on a bench and wiped off his neck and face as best he could. "So, any last terrorizing things you want to visit before we go to the country fair outside the gates and head home?"

Sarah Beth tilted her head, thinking. "Maybe that thing that drops you about five stories all at once."

"Yeah, I haven't ridden that in a long time," Sharon said, taking her hand.

Tanner groaned. "I'll just sit right here and dry out. You two have half an hour."

At the country fair they strolled, looked at crafts, and munched caramel apples. Sharon insisted on buying a stuffed-rabbit doll for Sarah Beth. It had a painted face, with hearts for cheeks, and a little calico dress.

"It will look good on your chest of drawers. And it's your birthday present."

"You didn't have to get me anything. Today was enough fun—I didn't need a present too," Sarah Beth told her. "But I love the bunny. Now I'll have to think about what to name her."

"You didn't have to," Tanner said softly

Kisses Worth Waiting For   121

as Sarah Beth walked in front of them. "But that was very kind. Thank you."

"I enjoy buying her things and doing things with her, Tanner. She needs another female person around some. I mean, you're an excellent father, but sometimes a girl's just got to be a girl."

"And you can facilitate that better than I can, huh?"

"Do you know she'd never read *Little Women* before? She told me she learned to read sitting on your lap with *Black's Law Dictionary.*"

"She did. Want to tell me it was bad for her? I dare you." Tanner's chin jutted out at an angle that made him all the more handsome.

"I couldn't tell you that. I'm just saying that once in a while she ought to have some female companionship."

"Her grandmother comes for a week every summer, never fails," he said. "And that . . . Ginger . . . seems to be a permanent fixture. Half the time when we get home, she's on the phone with her after supper, giggling and everything."

"Get used to it. You've only got another decade or so of that."

122   *Kisses Worth Waiting For*

"Great." He shook his head. "Just what I needed to hear. Does it get worse?"

"Has she started rolling her eyes when you talk to her, and speaking in very simple sentences so that you can understand her?" Sharon asked with a grin on her face.

He winced. "Not yet."

She put an arm around his waist for support. "It gets worse. Just ask my Aunt Betty sometime. She went through five teenagers and survived. Of course, she has snow-white hair. . . ."

Supper was at a roadside restaurant, where Tanner and Sharon both watched Sarah Beth put away fried chicken until they were amazed. "I mean, neither of us exactly picked at our food," he said, sipping his coffee. "Trooping around that place all day certainly built up an appetite. But honestly, Sarah Beth. . . ."

"I was hungry," she said, sipping up the last of her soda noisily through the straw and leaning back with a sigh. "And they have the best fried chicken here."

She looked at Sharon speculatively. "Can you fry chicken? Daddy can do a lot of cook-

Kisses Worth Waiting For   123

ing, but it's one of those things he can absolutely not do."

Sharon nodded. "I can fry chicken. Learned from my mom when I was about your age. If you want, I can come over some night and teach you, and then you can fry chicken."

"That would be cool. Except for that pie I baked with your mom, all I can do is brownies and nuclear stuff."

"Nuclear stuff?" Sharon was mystified.

Sarah Beth grinned. "You know, stuff you zap in the microwave."

"Okay, then, we'll make a date soon to learn the fine art of frying chicken."

"It's a deal," Sarah Beth said.

"I won't argue, either," Tanner put in. "In fact, give me a list, and I'll even buy the groceries."

"Spoken like a true gentleman."

"Yes, and put that purse away. True gentleman do not let ladies buy their own dinner or leave the tip. Keep it for next time."

"Fine. I'll bring flowers when I come fry chicken," Sharon said, feeling stubborn.

"You just do that. Anything but mums." Tanner helped her out of her chair, then went to pay the bill.

124   *Kisses Worth Waiting For*

"They make him sneeze," Sarah Beth whispered loudly.

"I'll remember," Sharon said, walking with her.

Sarah Beth reached up and companionably put an arm around her, and Sharon put one around her shoulders. They were bony and wider than she expected. She was growing up so fast.

Not for the first time Sharon wished she could watch this child grow all the time, perhaps even give her a family to grow up with. And for the first time ever, she didn't push the thought away as fast as it came.

Sarah Beth managed to stay awake the rest of the way home. Sharon wasn't sure how she did it. Her own head nodded a little once in a while in the fall twilight. It was nice to be in Tanner's car, listening to the two of them chat, the radio playing softly for background. Once again she felt like a family but pushed that thought away. It was far too soon to feel that way for Tanner's sake. For her own sake, she'd change their situation tomorrow if he were willing. Better to stay quiet and hope, she thought. Things were changing, and they'd keep changing. She

Kisses Worth Waiting For   125

smiled softly to herself, remembering her conversation with Sarah Beth in the restaurant in front of a mirror in the ladies' lounge.

"Do you like my dad, Sharon?"

"Of course I do. I wouldn't work with anybody for as many years as I have for your dad and not like him." She carefully blotted her lipstick, determined not to slip and say anything that would get Sarah Beth's hopes up.

"Good, because I think he likes you. I mean really *likes you,* you know?"

Sharon knew, but she didn't say much to Sarah Beth. It was enough to see the glow in her eyes.

The glow intensified when she saw the conference room. "All right. This is really neat." She looked up at the decorations, walked around the table, surveying the cake. "Got any matches? I want to make a wish before I blow them out."

Sharon lit the cake, and they watched Sarah Beth blow out the candles. She cut pieces of the cake for herself, Tanner, and Sharon. Tanner got three cans of soda out of the machine in the back hallway and came back.

"Your birthday celebration has been more

126   *Kisses Worth Waiting For*

like a week than a birth *day.* Better enjoy it, because it's not going to happen every year."

"That's okay." Sarah Beth stuck an icing-decorated finger into her mouth. "I had a good time with everything. I got to make wishes on two birthday cakes, and the first one has already come true."

"It wouldn't have been that bike you found in the garage about ten minutes after your first cake, would it?" Tanner asked, leaning back in his chair.

"Yeah. I think I may have to wait a little while longer for this one, though. Know what I wished?"

The moment seemed to freeze for Sharon. She could see a little breeze blowing the crepe paper above Sarah Beth's head, see the tendrils loosening from the glowing red braids. Watching her, she got a feeling like the one she'd had that afternoon on the highest loop of the Ninja, with her stomach dropping away from her.

"No, Peanut, what did you wish?" Tanner asked cheerfully.

"That we could keep having good times like today, Daddy. All the time." Sarah Beth's words were very deliberate as she looked straight at Tanner. "I mean, you like

Kisses Worth Waiting For 127

Sharon and she likes you, so I just wished you'd get married."

The words hung on the air as Tanner's cheer faded and he sat up in his chair. "Sarah Beth Williams, that is impossible. And I never want to hear about it again. I am perfectly serious. Not ever again, got it?"

The child could not have been more surprised if her father had slapped her. "Got it," she said with a gulp; then her eyes filled and she ran from the room.

Tanner stalked from the room after her, and Sharon was suddenly left alone.

Sharon looked at the ruins of the cake, crumbs around three paper plates, half-empty soda cans on the table. Slowly she picked up all the debris and took it to the dumpster in the back. Anything that would have reminded them of the day was removed from the conference room until it was clean and barren as usual, and Sharon felt exhaustion seep into her bones.

Dance is over, Cinderella, she told herself, locking the front door. If Tanner wanted silence on the issue, he'd get it from her.

Walking to her car, she nearly jumped out of her skin. There, leaning against the bumper, was Tanner. "I got a neighbor lady

128   *Kisses Worth Waiting For*

to sit downstairs in case Sarah Beth wakes up. I just couldn't leave you quite like I did."

"Well, that's mighty considerate, Tanner, but I understood your message just as clearly as Sarah Beth did. There's no need to elaborate." He reached out to take her arm, and Sharon wrenched away.

"Yes, there is," he said stubbornly. "I have to make sure she understands, Sharon, even if it hurts. No matter how much I love you, I am not marrying again. It wouldn't be fair for you, for her, for me."

"You mean, it wouldn't be convenient, don't you, Tanner?" Sharon snapped. "You've got your life all plotted out—hardworking attorney, noble single father, the whole bit. And letting me in might make you worry and hope and really feel something for a change. Well, if that's the way you want it, don't worry. I won't bother you again."

Sharon pulled the car door open, slammed it shut, and started the engine, leaving Tanner standing in a pool of light. For weeks that's how she thought of him, silhouetted in the pale yellow glow of the street lamp, looking lost and bewildered.

Chapter Eight

BY the following week Sharon was surprised to discover just how far two people in the same office complex could stay from each other. After a few days she was struck by something. It wasn't just two people. Sarah Beth hadn't been in the building for a week. She hadn't even trooped up the stairs to go to her father's office. It gave Sharon an extra nudge of pain to realize that. She had expected Tanner to stay far away from her after Saturday. That was no surprise. In fact, the only surprise there, she told herself, was that the final confrontation had taken that long.

After a few days of bruised feelings she had expected Sarah Beth back in the office, though. It just wasn't like her to stay away for a week. Maybe Tanner had told her not to come in. Sharon decided that if her absence lasted much longer, she'd swallow her pride and talk to Tanner. She wasn't about

130   *Kisses Worth Waiting For*

to let this deprive her of the company of both of the people she liked best to share her days with.

Not talking to Tanner was bad enough. All week she'd found herself throwing away half a pot of coffee at the end of the day because she'd automatically made enough for both of them. She had made a note to tell the cleaning service to stop using their new air freshener because everything smelled different in the hallways and conference area, and then she scratched the note. It wasn't a new air freshener that made things smell so flat . . . it was the absence of Tanner's cologne.

Lunch was downright boring, even if it was her week to cook. Sharon had eaten alone every day for a work week and discovered how much she had looked forward to Tanner's company. She'd joked with him, asked him questions about clients she found hard to solve herself, just enjoyed the noise of somebody else rattling waxed paper while she ate.

Driving home, Sharon thought. Maybe even if Sarah Beth came back, she'd have to speak to Tanner. She knew him well enough to predict that he'd never be the first one to

Kisses Worth Waiting For 131

break the ice. They'd spend their days in the same building, never saying another word to each other, if he had to be the first one to make friends again.

And she had to admit she wanted him as a friend. Not as much as she wanted him as many other things. She'd rather have Tanner as a friend with a matching gold band on his finger, a friend she could curl up next to during thunderstorms at midnight. But if Tanner was never going to be that kind of friend, the kind she'd known before would suffice. He was too good a person to throw out of her life totally just because he refused to admit he'd be better off marrying her and. . . .

She pounded on the steering wheel. "You're doing it again," she told herself out loud. "No more plans. No more dreams that include that man. No more." After all, they were hopeless, weren't they? She'd just have to be realistic and look for somebody else. Look hard this time until she found someone else.

The thought was so depressing she had to sit in her car with the keys in her hand for a while before she went inside the house. She didn't want India to see her like this again,

132   *Kisses Worth Waiting For*

looking droopy and wistful on the way into the house. If she came in that way, her sister would try to think of something for them to do or start calling her friends, organizing some kind of entertainment, and that was the last thing Sharon wanted right now.

What she wanted was exactly what she got. India was gone, working late to cover for somebody else, so Sharon fixed a solitary dinner, did some laundry, and wandered upstairs. The copy of *Little Women* that she'd lent to Sarah Beth was still on the dresser in the guest room. She leafed through it absently and wondered if there were any more of her books Sarah Beth would like to read.

Sharon was in the unfinished part of the attic, going through a trunk, when the phone rang. "How are you?" she asked all too heartily to the child on the other end of the line.

"Okay, I guess. But there's something I need to ask you," Sarah Beth said hesitantly.

"Go ahead," Sharon prompted.

"I guess there isn't, after all," the small voice on the other end said.

They talked for a few moments, about school and the office, and Sharon got the feeling that Sarah Beth was straining to

Kisses Worth Waiting For 133

make small talk. So she promised to bring in a book if she would stop by the office to pick it up.

"I will. Maybe next week," Sarah Beth promised before she hung up.

Sharon left the phone with a vague feeling that the conversation had all been a substitution for something else, something the girl had changed her mind about.

Shaking off her feelings of confusion, Sharon went back to the trunk. When she found the book she was looking for, she put it on the table near the front door, where she kept everything she wanted to take into work with her but would otherwise forget.

Then she spent the rest of the weekend keeping busy so that she could forget the sound of the small voice on the other end of her telephone and, more than that, forget the background noise that seemed to include music on the radio and a deep, rich baritone voice singing as someone did the dinner dishes.

Monday Sharon remembered the book, putting it on Anna Mae's desk with strict instructions that she should be interrupted if Sarah Beth came in to pick it up. Then she

134   *Kisses Worth Waiting For*

promptly got so busy, a herd of stampeding elephants couldn't have interrupted her.

Gnawing feelings in her stomach finally moved Sharon from her desk. Her coffee cup had been refilled several times during the day, but she'd never made it as far as the kitchen or the conference room to eat. She glanced at her watch. Three-thirty. "No place that has real table service will be open right now. Rats!" She headed to the kitchen to look at her lunch.

India was on another kick. There seemed to be a container of carrot soup and some very nutritious, uninteresting trail mix. Even Sharon was not that hungry. She rummaged in the pockets of her cardigan, hoping for an undiscovered piece of candy. Empty.

Then she remembered Anna Mae's private horde. There had to be frozen candy bars in the freezer compartment of the refrigerator. She opened it and nearly crowed with delight. "I'll pay you back later," she promised as she went past her cousin's desk, sinking her teeth into firm chocolate and nuts. It was heaven, even on a brisk November day.

"Chocolate is really good for what ails you," she told Jim as he stood up from the companion chair next to her desk. She was

Kisses Worth Waiting For   135

surprised when he didn't smile. He had always been the first to find any goodies she or anyone else had brought in when he'd interned in Tanner's office.

"Hey, I'll even share," she said lightly.

He shook his head. "I need to talk to you, Sharon. It's important. And serious."

"If it's financial, I'm sure we can work it out." She'd seen a few clients trickle into his office, and she was sure the trickle would increase before long. Nobody as personable and enthusiastic as Jim was going to stay idle long.

His serious look made her pause, brandishing her candy bar at him as she spoke. "But if this is another one of Tanner's schemes, you can tell him it won't work, James. I am not going to get involved with anything with you that will put us together for long hours."

Jim almost blushed. "So you caught on to that one, huh? Does that mean Anna Mae was just told to work with me and be nice?"

Sharon swallowed another bite of her delayed lunch. "No, she was just told to work with you. The being nice was her own idea."

Jim almost smiled. "Well, that's a relief. But I've still got problems. It's my latest cli-

136   *Kisses Worth Waiting For*

ent." The young lawyer looked more serious than she'd ever seen him, and Sharon began to wonder how hardened a criminal Cape Girardeau could possibly yield to make him look this troubled.

"Sarah Beth Williams."

"What?" Sharon just barely kept the candy bar from falling on the carpet. "Sarah Beth?"

Jim nodded, slumping in his chair. "She came to me straight after school today, bank-book in hand." He thrust a hand through his hair, disordering its careful cut. "She wants to sue her father."

This time the half of Sharon's candy bar that was left made it all the way to the floor. "Get comfortable, my friend," she told Jim. "I want to hear this story in detail, maybe more than once."

An hour and a half later the door to Tanner's office burst open. "Well, well, looks like a storm front," he said, trying to lighten the situation.

This time, Sharon told herself, it wasn't going to work.

He looked friendly enough, with his sleeves rolled up and papers spread over his

Kisses Worth Waiting For 137

desk. The office was quiet since there was no sound of Charlotte puttering in the next room. If she had seemed surprised by Sharon's telling her to leave early for home, she hadn't shown it. Sharon had worked for Tanner long enough herself to know that when anyone had offered her an early night off, she took the chance without being asked twice.

"We need to talk. Put down your pencil and get your coat. Now."

"I haven't seen you this steamed since I put the wrong stuff in the copy machine," Tanner said, still smiling that aggravating smile that crinkled up the skin around his bright eyes. Why did he have to look so appealing even when she was angry at him?

"I had every right to be mad. Nobody else would have thought that stuff you poured in was toner. That service call was higher than any office expense we had in six months except my salary, Tanner. But don't change the subject on me now. I'm serious."

"Oh, I'm fine, thanks. And Sarah Beth is too. I kind of expected her to come in today. She said something about a book," he said, acting as if the usual pleasantries had been exchanged.

138   *Kisses Worth Waiting For*

"Sarah Beth is not fine," Sharon countered, leaning over his desk.

The color left his face rapidly. "Has something happened?" He was standing and half into his coat in a split second.

"Nothing like you think. I called and made sure she could eat supper with Ginger and her family so you and I could have a little meeting."

"If she's all right, why did you scare me like that?" Tanner demanded angrily.

"Because I need to get through your thick skull," she said, standing before him. "Now let's get down to that conference room, and you get comfy, mister. Because we have plenty of talking to do."

Tanner started grinning when Sharon told him what Sarah Beth had done. By the time she was done, he was chuckling. "Even Sarah Beth ought to know you can't sue somebody for alienation of affection anymore. That's archaic."

"Tanner, this is serious. You may be amused, but I'm not. She is perfectly serious." Sharon tried hard not to shriek at him while she made him see how she felt. "Think, Tanner, really think. You are the person she loves best in the whole world, and she's try-

Kisses Worth Waiting For   139

ing to sue you. She offered Jim all the money in her bankbook. He doesn't know what to do."

"Charge her a retainer. It would teach her a lesson."

This time Sharon took him by the shoulders, shaking him out of his comfortable posture in the conference chair. "You are tearing that little girl's world apart, Tanner Williams. I want you to go home tonight and tell her how much you love her. Then I want you to explain to her in words she can understand exactly why you aren't going to marry me. I may even go along just to hear what you say to her so I know what to say afterward."

"And you think that will make her happy?" There was a crease in Tanner's forehead.

"No. It won't make any of us happy. But it will keep her from trying to sue you. Has she been unhappy at home?"

"Mostly just quiet. In fact, until I really considered it just now, I hadn't realized how quiet," he said thoughtfully.

"And answer a foolish question for me. Is that normal for Sarah Beth?"

Tanner's eyes sparkled. "I think this is

140   *Kisses Worth Waiting For*

called leading the witness, Sharon. Of course that's not normal. I should have picked up on it myself. I guess I appreciate your bringing me back down to earth like this. Are you sure you want to come home with me?"

"Positive." It wouldn't be pretty, but it had to be done, Sharon told herself.

"What do you think you're going to hear?"

"You, of course. Telling Sarah Beth why you're not getting married and why she can't sue you."

"Keep going," he said, watching her ease into the chair next to him.

"I expect I'll hear what I've known all along," she continued, trying to keep calm, willing her voice not to waver. "You really loved Tory. And I'm not up to replacing her. Maybe nobody is. But, Tanner, Sarah Beth needs to hear that, so she can stop her daydreams about us. Heck, maybe I need to hear it so I can stop mine—" she blurted out.

"Do you? Have daydreams, I mean. About us?" Tanner's face held a look Sharon had never seen and couldn't quite fathom.

She looked away from him. "I guess I do. Or at least did. It's hard to work next to somebody as good-looking and interesting as

Kisses Worth Waiting For   141

you for as long as I have without some feelings, Tanner. Surely you know that."

His hair was falling over his forehead in disarray, and his eyes held a look that was sweet, almost bemused. "Tell me."

"Why? So I can hear you tell me again how foolish I am? So I can hear that I just don't measure up?" Sharon held onto the arms of her chair, fighting tears.

In an instant his arm was around her, strong, comforting. "Oh, Sharon, is that really the way you feel? I know I've told you I'd never marry again. And Tory was a very special person, a sweet and vital part of my youth." So close to him, Sharon saw the set of his jaw harden and a little muscle twitch. "You couldn't ever replace her. People don't replace people, Sharon. But that's not why I'd never marry again."

"It . . . it . . . isn't?"

Tanner shook his head. This close it was all Sharon could do to keep her fingers from reaching out and stroking the spot right at his temple where a pulse throbbed and the tiniest bit of gray streaked the chestnut hair.

"Tory was loving and patient and kind. And I put her through hell. The best place we ever lived was a third-floor apartment

142   *Kisses Worth Waiting For*

with bedrooms the size of closets and no air conditioning. I can't even count the house. She never lived there long enough to enjoy it."

He paused for a moment and seemed to gulp for air, then continued. "She worked long hours to put me through school and stayed home even longer hours alone with an infant while I built a practice."

He turned to face Sharon head on. "My life hasn't changed all that much. When I'm in the middle of a big case, I'm grumpy and irascible. I'll never be a millionaire despite what you've heard about rich lawyers. And for weeks at a time I'm not home much."

"And even when you're home, you're not home, if your behavior in the office is any indication. Your brain is still down at the courthouse," Sharon said softly.

"So if you know that already, can't you understand what I'm telling you?"

Tanner looked pained, and this time Sharon didn't control the impulse to reach out and smooth his face between her hands.

"No, Tanner, I can't. I know all that about you. I have from the day I walked into your office and answered your ad for a secretary. I think I loved you even then, even

Kisses Worth Waiting For   143

though you were the worst interviewer I'd ever seen. Is this what you're trying to tell me? That you couldn't marry me because you're not marriage material?"

"I guess so. Do you think you could stop doing that?"

"Why? Don't you like it?"

"No. I mean yes, I like it a lot. And it's terribly distracting."

"Good," she said, continuing to stroke his temples, his forehead, and moving down the firm column of his neck. "Then I'll keep doing it while I tell you why I am not going to give up on you. And why we are going to go to your house, together, and talk to Sarah Beth and explain why she can't sue you."

"Which is?"

"Because there's been no alienation of affection. I love you, Tanner. I have for years, and I will as long as I draw breath. And I want to give that love a chance. Will you let me?"

Tanner's answer was a kiss that made Sharon's head spin. In a moment she was enveloped by him, the nubby texture of his jacket pressed against her skin, the feel of his lips on hers, the outdoor scent of his cologne filling her senses every time she drew breath.

144   *Kisses Worth Waiting For*

"I'll try," he said when he drew back long enough to look into her face. "It won't be easy."

"If it were easy, do you think either of us would be interested long?" she asked before she returned his kiss.

The lights in the conference room were on a very long time. And afterward, at Tanner's house, Sarah Beth was up long past her bedtime as the three of them talked. Late that night, when Sharon finally made it home, she realized she hadn't eaten since the half a candy bar in the middle of the afternoon.

She was suddenly ravenously hungry and jubilant at the same time, with energy to burn. When India stumbled into the kitchen later, tousled and confused, she took one look at Sharon and laughed. "I cannot imagine why anyone would fry chicken and bake biscuits at this time of the night, but I'm game to help you get rid of the results."

"It isn't a private party," Sharon said, laughing. "Pull up a chair and I'll tell you a story."

"Is it a good one?"

"Complete with happy ending. Find the butter and the honey, will you?" Sharon said.

Kisses Worth Waiting For   145

If anyone next door at the big house noticed the midnight reveling, they had the grace to keep quiet about it. Doing the dishes, Sharon watched a falling star. For the first time in years she couldn't think of a wish to make upon it. There was nothing left to wish for that wasn't within her grasp. It was hard not to sing out loud as she went in to bed.

Chapter Nine

"TELL me again how I got talked into this," Tanner asked Sharon as he straightened his tie outside the entrance to the large hall. Even though it was barely March, he looked uncomfortably warm. Sharon suspected it had less to do with the weather, which was springlike, than with the concentration of Mumfords on the other side of the wall.

"It's simple, darling," she said, smoothing his jacket lapels for him. "You merely said in front of my mother what you said so many times to me, that no one could possibly have as many cousins as I do. And, being a lady of great dignity, she decided to prove to you that you were sadly mistaken."

"So now I'm going to be spending an entire afternoon and evening in the company of over a hundred people—"

"One hundred and sixty-eight, not includ-

147

148   *Kisses Worth Waiting For*

ing spouses and dates, at last count," Sharon added helpfully.

"As I said, over one hundred people I do not know from Adam, or Eve as the case may be, all of whom are allegedly Mumfords."

"That about sizes it up. Perhaps in the future you will be more careful what you say around the Mumfords, anyway. And, Tanner, you do know a few of them. You know Kathleen and Matt, and you know Ed, who put in our air conditioning in the building last summer, and—"

"And they will be but faces in a sea of Mumfords," Tanner muttered. "Well, let's get this over with."

Sarah Beth, walking behind them, wasn't as apprehensive as her father, Sharon noted. She was bouncing with excitement. Missy had promised to meet her early in the day and introduce her to all the girls that traveled in the large pack of like-aged cousins.

She scooted in the door ahead of them, running over to Missy, who stood inside the second set of double doors, scouting for Sarah Beth.

"Probably the last we'll see of her until at least dinnertime," Sharon told Tanner.

Kisses Worth Waiting For   149

"Now why don't we introduce you to a few folks?"

An hour later Tanner was sitting at a table with Sharon, sipping a cool drink. His suit coat had gone the way of most of the men's and been hung on one of the metal racks provided by the Elks Lodge, owners of the hall. His shirtsleeves were rolled up, and Sharon noted that he was actually smiling.

"Think you'll live?"

He slipped an arm around her and grinned. "Oh, I know I will. Lawyers seem to be a fairly rare commodity among the Mumfords. And the few that there are appear to practice in far-flung locations. In the past hour alone I have told three different people to call me Monday at the office. Business is booming."

Sharon raised an eyebrow, and gave Tanner what she hoped was an imperious look. "Nepotism? Why, Tanner! And all these new clients seem to be named Mumford. How can that be? Surely nobody could have that many cousins!"

He held up a palm. "All right, I concede defeat. You do have that many cousins. And a fine bunch of people they are too. However,

150   *Kisses Worth Waiting For*

I haven't seen many yet who would rival the future Mrs. Williams in looks."

"Don't say that too loudly," Sharon said, slipping fingers over his mouth gently, then taking them away.

"What, that I think you're the most beautiful lady here? Surely your mother wouldn't dispute me on that one?"

"Not at all. But that future Mrs. Williams stuff . . . I mean, we haven't made it official or anything."

"Only because you keep saying it's too soon for me to slip a ring on you," Tanner argued. "A fact which my daughter reminds me of as often as possible. Come on, Sharon. I'm not a kid anymore. Let's set a date while I can still remember my wedding anniversary without too many prompts, okay?"

He pulled her down, gently, to his knee, and Sharon didn't protest. Her family was used to seeing her with Tanner, and they were hardly the only couple in the room slipping off from time to time for some private conversation and perhaps a quick hug. Family reunions, with their closeness and excitement, seemed to bring that out in many of the couples.

"I don't know," she told Tanner truth-

Kisses Worth Waiting For 151

fully. "I hate to rush into things. Let's face it, Tanner, I still keep thinking this is all a wonderful dream and I'm going to wake up and you'll change your mind."

"Not a chance." He pulled her even closer. "After all, I survived a Turner-Mumford Christmas. I figure if I can live through that, I can handle anything you all can dish out."

"I like our Christmases," Sharon said, drawing her lips into a small pout. "Just because you're used to something more sedate. . . ."

"Just less like the middle of a hurricane. I've never heard so much whooping and ripping of paper and scrunching of boxes in my life."

"Now, we all knew what we were doing. I know, you're used to quiet little get-togethers in front of the tree, cups of eggnog balanced on your knee, and your mother sitting and handing out each present, one by one. But, Tanner, let's face it. If we tried it that way with our mob, between all of Aunt Betty's kids and the grandkids and all of us, somebody wouldn't get his last present until New Year's Eve."

He nodded. "You're right. Which is why

152   *Kisses Worth Waiting For*

I wouldn't want you to change your traditions for the world. But to an outsider, they are a little . . . rambunctious."

"Agreed. And I do like it," she said, slipping off his lap and standing up. "Secretly I think you would admit you liked it too."

"Once I could hear out of both ears again, I loved it. And Sarah Beth was in heaven. Which reminds me, have you seen her lately?"

"Nope." Sharon cocked her head. "Listen for high-pitched giggling and shrieking. I seem to remember that is what designates the corner where the girls her age hang out. Somewhere near where the band will set up later." Sharon craned her neck, standing on tiptoe. "I hear them, but I can't see them."

Tanner stood behind her, gently bridging his fingers and leaning on the top of her head. "That is the advantage of height. Now, knowing where to look, I can see them. Sarah Beth is in the middle of about eight or nine little girls, all of them giggling and whispering. She's perfectly happy, so I'm not going to interrupt."

Sharon leaned back against him, treasuring the feel of his solid chest against her back. "So what are you going to do instead?"

Kisses Worth Waiting For   153

"Check out the wall of fame, or whatever it is over there," he said, motioning. "Some of those clippings and old family-history things looked interesting."

"Fine. I've seen most of them. Mind if I go check in the kitchen to see how things are coming?"

"Go ahead. I'll know where to find you later."

It was warm in the kitchen, but not overly so. The sounds and smells and feel of it all felt like a giant hug. Sharon could smell cinnamon, and roast beef simmering in gravy somewhere. Aunt Betty was making a crock of iced tea that must have held ten gallons.

Standing next to her and talking, Sharon sliced lemons to go alongside. She admired a few new Mumford babies, including one very bald young man who smiled at everyone, rolling around in his walker, crowing wildly with each new skirt hem or pant leg he could capture.

Kathleen had come in, taking her ribbing from the older female members of the Mumford clan, in charge of the cooking as usual. "She's been married over a year. It's not too soon to ask if I'm going to be a great-aunt,"

154 *Kisses Worth Waiting For*

one of the women called, laughing at Kathleen's blush.

"Oh, leave her be," Sharon said good-naturedly. "Give her a little more time to be a newlywed."

Kathleen winked at her and mouthed a silent thank-you. She joined Sharon stirring the contents of several of the large pots simmering on the burners in a corner away from most of the commotion. "Confidentially, I think by the next Mumford family reunion there is going to be another Mumford, but I'm not telling anybody else until after Christmas," Kathleen said, eyes glowing. "Think there's room in that corner of my office where the chair is now for a port-a-crib?"

"Plenty," Sharon said, giving her a quick hug. "And enough of us around that you'll always have help. Go for it, Kathleen."

On the edges of her hearing, Sharon realized that the older members of the clan were now discussing the possible partners some of the younger Mumfords had brought to the reunion. They approved of Tanner. Sharon tried not to blush as they dissected his finer characteristics and pronounced him adequate if not better.

Kisses Worth Waiting For   155

His good looks won him a lot of compliments, to the point that several great-aunts wished they were at least twenty years younger. Sharon made a note to tell Tanner to dance with at least one of them after dinner and the roll call. That would put him on their favorite list until the year 2000. Sharon's mother had nice things to say about him that won all the other ladies' hearts, especially when she told them that he'd showed up for chicken-frying lessons along with his daughter.

In a bit Tanner came in himself and dropped a kiss on Sharon's forehead. "You look good in an apron. I ought to get a picture," he teased.

"Go right ahead." She grinned. "I like being in an apron once in a while. Especially here. You okay?"

He seemed distracted as he looked out the broad pass-through into the main room. "Just fine. Thinking about something I read, is all. That man over there asked me if I wanted to run for lieutenant governor," he said, bemused. He pointed to an older gentleman with a broad forehead, jaunty straw hat, and long white beard.

"Lieutenant governor? You ought to feel

156   *Kisses Worth Waiting For*

honored. I don't ever remember Cousin Carney asking anybody to run for any office higher than attorney general on his ticket in years. Has he, Mom?"

"Not that I can remember, not since Grandpa. That was the year they got eight hundred and fifty-seven votes statewide."

Sharon couldn't resist the hoot of laughter that bubbled up at Tanner's look of amazement. "You mean he actually runs?" he blurted out.

"Every time. He says it keeps the system honest. Runs on the Independent ticket, every gubernatorial primary there is. Never gets elected, but he says it doesn't matter. He just runs because it's the American thing to do."

Tanner looked back at the old gentleman. "And here I turned him down. Wait until Sarah Beth hears that. She'll tell me I made a mistake."

Sharon hugged him. "Dinner's almost ready. You want to find her and see if she wants to eat with us or with her new cousin-friends?"

"Will do. Don't be surprised if we lose out," he said.

"I won't. I'm just glad she's having a good

Kisses Worth Waiting For   157

time. I can remember being her age at Mumford reunions. It was always a day of great happenings. I'm happy that it can be that way for somebody else."

Sharon watched Sarah Beth as Tanner walked toward her. Unaware of anyone observing her but her newfound friends, Sarah Beth was a picture. She wore a dress in a pretty floral print that India had insisted she try on at the mall one night. Her usual braids had been traded for a ponytail caught up in a large bow, and she fairly glowed. Sharon felt a warmth when she looked at her, glad to have a part in watching her grow and seeing her bask in her father's love.

There was so much love in him to give. Sharon was amazed that she had ever found him close with his emotions. Since fall, he had been pressing her to set a wedding date. But, having waited so long for him, Sharon wanted to savor their romance—and, also, she wanted to be sure that he truly knew what he wanted. So she had held back about setting a date—and he had intensified his campaign to get her to the altar. She was always finding flowers and notes on her desk, or funny little limericks. Often he came to get her for lunch, surprising her with a hug

158   *Kisses Worth Waiting For*

before she knew he was there. For a tall man he was quiet on his feet, and more often than not her reading glasses landed in her lap when Tanner came up behind her.

He came up behind Sarah Beth now but made plenty of noise so he wouldn't interrupt anything that was happening with her friends. Sharon saw their heads bent together in conversation, then saw Sarah Beth smile, hug him quickly, and go back to the girls. Sharon sighed. She was going to have to eat one-handed. Without Sarah Beth there to tease him a little, Tanner would hold her hand all through dinner.

"All right, Tanner, give me my hand back and let me drink my coffee in peace," Sharon told him after the long, leisurely meal. It was nice to sit here, with Tanner beside her and her family all around her.

Cousin Ed was going to the podium now to start the annual counting of the Mumfords. He had inherited the job from his grandfather a couple of years back and did it with great style and flourish.

"Ladies and gentlemen, boys and girls, it is now time for the annual count. We have a few prizes to give away first. The farthest

Kisses Worth Waiting For   159

arrival this year goes to Florence Mumford of Oakland, California." There was applause, and Florence came up to accept her award.

"Oldest Mumford again goes to Edna Mae Mumford Smith, ninety-eight and four months. Edna could not be with us today because she's staying home with her daughter, who broke her hip."

"There's some perverse humor in there somewhere, but you'll kill me if I laugh," Tanner whispered, tickling Sharon's ear.

"You're right. Now be good and listen." She slipped her arm around him and leaned on his shoulder.

"Youngest Mumford goes to Jeffrey Mumford, thirty-eight days. He is here with his parents, who just happen to be my son Ed, Junior, and his lovely wife, Kate, of Sikeston." There was applause again, and Ed and Jeffrey came up to accept their prize.

"And now, down to the serious business. We are now ready to count the descendants of the original Mumford clan who came to settle this area from the hills of Kentucky in the last century. Will all descendants of Bartholomew please gather in the far-south corner?"

160   *Kisses Worth Waiting For*

There was a pushing back of chairs and a moving of people, and several dozen folks moved into a friendly group in the corner. Designated counters were busy for a moment, then someone called out, "Thirty-nine people, babes in arms included, Ed. All descendants of Bartholomew Mumford have been counted."

"Great. Now we have the descendants of Sarah Mumford Hughes. Any descendants of Sarah please go to the far-north corner."

"She always has the most," Sharon said. "But someday old Nate's tribe is going to beat her out."

Tanner raised an eyebrow. "That, I take it, is your branch of the family?"

"Definitely. And it's almost our time to be counted. See you in a minute."

Ed called for descendants of Nathaniel Mumford, and Sharon's table and those around her milled into their spot. "Forty-two," she said when she came back. "Just three more and we've got Sarah licked."

"Well, see now, if you'd just marry me and we got busy, we could contribute to the total by the next reunion," Tanner said, eyes gleaming.

Kisses Worth Waiting For   161

"I'll consider it," Sharon told him. "Just don't hold your breath waiting."

"And now, for my annual exercise in futility," Ed announced, which was followed by laughter. "Will all descendants of Julia Naomi Mumford Burrows Fielding—"

"Add another Fielding in there," somebody hooted.

". . . Fielding Morrow may stand in the middle of the room. And since there are none—"

"Now hang on a minute. Tanner looks interested in this," Sharon called. "Go through the whole thing for a change, will you?"

"Right," Kathleen chorused. "Matt hasn't heard the spiel, either."

"If you insist," Ed said. "Our dear, beloved Julia is somewhat of a legend among the Mumfords. At one time she could have gone to five family reunions all by herself. After her first husband, Mr. Burrows, met his demise, the widow took her two lovely daughters and married a Mr. Tad Fielding. Mr. Fielding, it seems, was no luckier than Mr. Burrows and soon went to his reward, not before adding a son to the flock and asking his brother Clarence to look after dear

162   *Kisses Worth Waiting For*

Julia. Clarence then married dear Julia, and several more children ensued, one of whom passed on, along with his father, in a smallpox epidemic. Julia's history gets a little cloudy at that point, but it seems she recovered sufficiently in several years to wed a Mr. Abraham Morrow, who had the unbelievable luck of outliving her."

Tanner stood up, and Sharon noticed that he looked a little pale. "Mr. Mumford, I think I can clarify the cloudy part of Julia's history. Between Mr. Fielding the second and Mr. Morrow there was another marriage."

"Oh?" Cousin Ed looked over his spectacles.

"Yes. To a Mr. Garth Williams, who happens to be my great-grandfather. We always had a bit of trouble tracing Great-grandmother's family tree, and now I know why. Add another boy and two girls in there too."

"That would be Anna, Elizabeth, and Tanner?"

Tanner nodded.

Ed chuckled. "We always wondered where they came from. Figured they were just stepchildren she'd picked up somewhere along the way."

Kisses Worth Waiting For 163

"Tanner, does this mean what I think it does?" Sharon asked, trying hard not to giggle.

Sarah Beth was bouncing beside her father. "It means that Daddy was wrong. He said nobody could have this many cousins. And now *I* have this many cousins!"

"Cousin Tanner!" Kathleen exclaimed, getting up to put an arm around him. "Welcome to the family."

"Go stand in the center of the room, Sarah Beth," Tanner said. "We're about to make history. Your father is going to have to eat his words."

"So is it really such a terrible thing, having this many cousins?" Sharon asked late that night as they sat in Tanner's living room, sipping a glass of wine.

"Not when you're one of them. Now, this won't be an argument for you to go weaseling out of marrying me, will it?"

"Tanner, we've got to be thirty-seventh cousins twice removed, or some such," Sharon said. "I don't think it matters."

"It matters to me. Suddenly I have this huge family I never knew existed."

"Yeah, and all of them will want legal

164   *Kisses Worth Waiting For*

services at some time or another, so be prepared!"

Tanner raised his glass. "To Julia. And to
cousins. Especially kissing cousins." The
glass chimed as the wine glasses touched
each other; then he pulled her close for an
embrace. "To kissing one cousin, actually.
A thirty-seventh cousin twice removed. But
not too far removed. I want you close
enough so that I can run my hands through
that glossy hair." His kiss tasted of wine,
full-bodied and sweet.

Chapter Ten

SHARON stood in front of the mirror set up in the ladies' room of the church, adjusting the ruffles on the deep neckline of her ivory dress.

"Are you sure about this, India? I told you before I'm just not the glamorous type. Don't I look silly in this?"

India came over, floating in her own deep-rose dress. "Not at all. You're just nervous. Here, let me stand here and get it all smoothed out. You'll see. It will look just fine."

She bent over Sharon, tucking, tugging, and fussing like a mother hen. When she stood aside, Sharon looked in the mirror again and smiled. India was right. The dress was grand but not overdone. The warm ivory satin glowed back at her from her reflection. "Now all we need to do is get your gloves and your wreath on," India told her.

"Not yet. We still have an hour before the

166   *Kisses Worth Waiting For*

ceremony, and I know that Tanner is going to fall apart sometime before then. I'm staying right here to pick up the pieces."

"If you say so," India said. "You would know better than anybody. But if you see him before the wedding, Mama's going to have a fit."

Mrs. Turner came in, smiling broadly and leading Sarah Beth by the hand. "Now, doesn't she look beautiful?"

Sharon could tell that her mother had spent the last hour fussing over Sarah Beth as India had fussed over her. There were waves and curls cascading down her back, caught by a headband wrapped in flowers and lace. Her dress was a miniature of India's, in pale spring green.

"You look beautiful, Sarah Beth. But then I think you look beautiful in blue jeans and that awful shirt you wear to school every Friday," Sharon said, tracing a finger down her nose.

Sarah Beth giggled. "I like that shirt. Just because it has a couple of holes in it from where I climbed that fence is no reason to get rid of it. After all, Daddy still has that old Mizzou sweatshirt he mows the lawn in. Do you know that before you guys got en-

Kisses Worth Waiting For   167

gaged, he used to wear it inside the house sometimes? All day?"

"I'm glad he gave that up," Sharon said, trying to suppress a shudder. "I'd never throw it out, but I'd hate to have to live with it forever, either."

"Forever," Sarah Beth caroled. "Doesn't that sound nice? You're going to come and stay forever." She sobered up a little. "Or at least as close to forever as we can manage, right?"

"Right. You'll leave home before I will, Sarah Beth. We'll pack you and forty-seven boxes off for college, and your father will complain about how many pairs of shoes you're taking."

Sarah Beth giggled again. "I'm going to go and see how he's doing."

"All right, but remember to knock first, okay?"

"Okay." She was off with a briskly closed door, and Sharon could hear her going up the hall at a rapid pace. It was almost as rapid as her own heartbeat was becoming.

This was it, her wedding day. There hadn't been any fireworks when she got up that morning, just a regular old sunrise. She had stripped her bed methodically and put

the sheets next to the washing machine for
India. Her closet looked so empty, with most
of the things already at Tanner's and what
was left packed in the two little suitcases
they were taking on their honeymoon. It was
strange to think that tomorrow they'd be
leaving the big brick house and going off together, married.

He had offered to sell the house and find
a new one, but Sharon had refused. "This is
your home. And I want it to be my home,
too, Tanner. There's no need to uproot the
two of you. I think I can fit in here just fine,
unless it bothers you."

"I thought about it quite a while after you
finally said you'd marry me, after the reunion," Tanner said. "And to me, this was
never Tory's house. She never got to stay
long enough to put her mark on it. So if it
doesn't bother you, it certainly won't bother
me." He had stayed quiet for a while; then
a grin spread over his face.

"No, I certainly don't want to move. I've
had too many fantasies about your standing
in the kitchen in the morning in a cotton
nightgown. The window is open just a little,
the breeze has caught the hem, and you're
standing at the stove, minding some bacon

and eggs. Maybe you're so intent on watching them, you might not hear me when I come down the stairs." He nuzzled her neck to illustrate his point.

"I hope reality is as good as your dreams, Tanner. Just think about what you're letting yourself in for. Two females in your happy home every morning. Dripping panty hose suspended in the shower, makeup on the vanity, nail-polish searches. . . ."

"I can hardly wait." He actually smiled while he said it.

"Are you sure? I'm a little, well . . . fuzzy . . . in the morning. Ask Sarah Beth. She's spent a couple of weekends out in Scott City now. She can tell you."

"Oh, she has, in detail. I'm very thankful we have two full bathrooms so that I can install your makeup mirror in one of them. According to her, we'll need that. But I'm still looking forward to waking up in the morning and seeing you, fuzzy or not."

"I'm glad. Guess I ought to ask Sarah Beth what you're like in the morning. I mean, by the time I see you at work, you've had a shower and breakfast. . . ."

"And coffee. Plenty of coffee." Tanner's smile was blissful. "I just realized that if I marry you and I'm very, very nice to you, I'll get your wonderful coffee every morning. Maybe mornings won't be so grim, after all."

"I'll try to make it as pleasant as possible," Sharon had promised.

It was the least she could do, she reasoned. After all, Tanner was being so pleasant about everything. The wedding plans had started out simply. They had just snowballed little by little.

It was hard to have a quiet engagement when you had dozens of cousins and an entire courthouse wanting all the details. Sharon knew things were getting way out of hand when the municipal courts got together and gave them a couples shower.

The cousins didn't bother with a regular shower. They just all started offering things to Tanner and Sharon instead. This time Tanner didn't protest. "Now that I'm living proof that you can have one hundred and nineteen cousins, I might as well be gracious about it all," he said as the gifts started pouring in.

Most of them weren't your run-of-the-mill wedding gifts. Ordinary or not, almost all of them were coming in handy.

Kathleen used her contacts at the best

Kisses Worth Waiting For   171

printer in town to get them free invitations. "And as a present I'm giving you napkins for the reception," she told Sharon.

When she looked at the sample, Sharon's eyes misted. Seeing her name linked with Tanner's on everything caused that reaction each and every time.

It happened when the etched silver trays and the hand-stitched samplers came in to her mother's house. It happened with the more offbeat gifts, like Cousin Ed's offering to upgrade the heating system at Shalimar. It even happened when Sarah Beth gave them her gift, a handmade coupon book promising a clean room, folded laundry, and all dinner dishes done for a month.

Sharon had hugged her, tightly, so that she wouldn't see the tears threatening for a few moments. "Don't you know that you are your own present, Sarah Beth? I'm so happy that we're going to be a family, you don't have to give us anything."

"I'll second that motion," Tanner had said. "Of course, if you're offering to clean your room, I'll still take you up on it. . . ."

Sharon looked at Sarah Beth now, standing in front of her, their reflections in the mirror still and calm. They looked much

172 *Kisses Worth Waiting For*

more peaceful than she suspected either of them felt. "Just think, next time you look at yourself like this, you'll be married. Are you scared, Sharon?"

"A little bit. Not of getting married, but just of getting today over with, I guess. I mean, what if I trip on my dress?"

"Too short," Sarah Beth countered practically. "Ballerina length cannot be tripped on."

"True. But what if my wreath blows off, or I say the wrong words, or I get tickled and get the giggles or something?"

Sarah Beth hugged her carefully, so as not to smash any of the ruffles of lace. "You won't. Your wreath will stay on, Reverend Perkins will help you with the words, and you only get tickled when Daddy and Shane both start teasing you at once. And today Daddy's too nervous, and I told Shane I'd kick him in the shins if he even thought about it. After that last touch-football game he knows I'd do it, too, so he'll be good."

Sharon laughed, the first time all day. "My heroine. Is your dad really that nervous?"

Sarah Beth nodded, eyes twinkling. "He should be down here anytime now, I think.

Kisses Worth Waiting For   173

Neither he nor Jim could get that tie tied. Bet he comes down here calling you in about thirty seconds."

It took about forty-five.

And, as promised, Sharon's mother was flustered. "I should have made you dress at home, where this couldn't happen."

"My dress would have been squashed flat on the ride up from Scott City," Sharon argued. She stepped around her mother to open the door and go out in the hall to Tanner.

He looked extremely relieved to see her. "Help me get this tie together. It won't tie, and we're going to be late."

Sharon's mother tried to shoo him away. "Don't you know it's bad luck to visit with the bride before the wedding?"

"No such thing," Tanner said. "My luck has been great since the day she finally agreed to marry me. Nothing is going to change that now. Besides, we haven't done one blasted thing in this entire relationship traditionally. Why should we start now?"

"Suit yourselves. I'm going to make sure everything's gathered up here and India and Sarah Beth are all ready. I expect you two in ten minutes, tops, or I'm coming back to

174   *Kisses Worth Waiting For*

get you." Mrs. Turner closed the door, leaving them alone in the echoing hallway.

Sharon busied herself tying the recalcitrant tie. "There. Fixed. Now, just don't put your finger under your collar and loosen it up, okay?"

"Okay. Can I kiss you or anything without destroying that beautiful makeup job?"

"Not wearing any, except for a little bit of lip gloss, and I can always retouch that," Sharon said, coming as close into his arms as she dared in her full skirt.

"Just the natural glow of a happy bride," Tanner murmured, settling his arms around her. "You are, aren't you? Happy, I mean? No regrets?"

"None. Except maybe that we didn't do this sooner. But I wouldn't miss this day for the world."

"Me neither, now that it's here. Judge McCabe is still mad at us for not getting married in his courtroom."

"I like this church," Sharon said firmly. "I'm looking forward to coming back here every Sunday morning with my husband and daughter. Gee, that has a nice ring to it, doesn't it?"

Tanner smiled. "It does. Guess we'd bet-

Kisses Worth Waiting For   175

ter get the show on the road, or your mother's going to come back out here and start clucking at us. She's sure we're going to be late for our own wedding, isn't she?"

"Consider your track record, Tanner. Christmas morning you pulled up forty-five minutes after you said you would, you've been in court twice when you were supposed to be at her dinner table, you're eternally losing your concentration in the middle of a conversation and wandering off to thoughts of some case or another. . . ."

"Okay, I admit it. You're the one who keeps me on track. See? After today I guess that means I'll always be on time."

"No, it just means I'll know why you aren't," Sharon said, grinning. "Come on, go find Jim and Shane and pretend you haven't seen me, okay?"

"One important thing first. I want to kiss a single lady one last time and see if it's any different." He leaned toward her, and his lips met hers in the softest, gentlest of kisses. It deepened as she moved toward him, and one of his hands settled above the sloping shoulder of her gown, caressing the warm skin there and making her suppress a shiver. "Same as always, just wonderful," he said

176   *Kisses Worth Waiting For*

when he drew back, eyes aglow. "We'll try it again in an hour or so and see what kissing a married lady is like."

The hallway leading to the sanctuary of the church seemed much longer than it had at the rehearsal. Sharon's father was there beside her, making sure she managed the full skirt all right. The look in his eyes said that Tanner better mind his business around him for the first few months. Sharon knew her father wasn't completely sure that twenty-six was old enough to get married. She suspected that an announcement that they'd decided to spare his oldest daughter for another decade or so might have been fine with him.

"Need a cool drink or anything?"

"No drinks, no airplane tickets out of town, nothing, Dad," Sharon said, a note of teasing in her voice. "Just a hand to lean on while I get one wrinkle out of my hose."

She did lean on him while she smoothed the nylon at her ankle. Then she slipped the satin pump back on and smiled at him. "Let's get settled, then find the florist and get our flowers. If we don't do it soon, Mom will send out the search party."

Kisses Worth Waiting For 177

"You know that she will," her father agreed.

The florist helped him pin on his bouton-niere and handed Sharon her bouquet. Inside the church Shane walked her mother down the aisle. Sharon was sure her mother was already reaching for the linen hanky in her purse.

Sharon knew it was a different sort of wedding than the Reverend Perkins usually saw. There weren't normally banks of potted flowers in the room, courtesy of a cousin who ran a nursery over near Jackson and wanted to provide some nice flowers they could use in the yard afterward. Most couples did not bring their own orchestra of keyboard, guitar, and singers to the wedding to supplement the church organ, but when you had such talented musical relatives, it just happened naturally, Sharon mused.

Thinking about them playing up in the loft made her less skittish as she grasped her father's arm and looked at Tanner in the front by the altar. He was her anchor, the thing that kept her from getting really nervous. All she had to do was remind herself that this was what today was all about and look at the

178   *Kisses Worth Waiting For*

warm, happy glow in those gray eyes and she stopped shaking.

The ceremony was a little bit of a blur for her. She knew that she said all the words right, and the ring went from India's hand to hers to Tanner's finger without being dropped. Her own ring slid from Jim's pocket to Tanner's hand to hers with no mishaps. And she was sure that Reverend Perkins's talk was lovely. She just couldn't remember much more than the promises Tanner seemed to be speaking with his eyes, and that, Sharon told herself, was the important part, anyway.

When Reverend Perkins told him he could kiss the bride, Tanner picked her up gently, kissed her thoroughly, and set her down after a half turn. "Even better than a single lady," he whispered in her ear as he walked her down the smiling rows of cousins.

Outside in the sunshine they had an informal receiving line full of courthouse employees, cousins, and plenty of others. There, finally, the spring breeze tugged Sharon's wreath nearly off, and she had to keep one hand on it, letting go only for tight hugs for favorite cousins.

After a hearty kiss for the bride, Judge

Kisses Worth Waiting For 179

McCabe complimented them on the ceremony. "Almost as nice as I could have done myself," he said. "But then, I guess one of the party's leading candidates for my job when I retire in two years has to do it up right."

"You, a judge?" Sharon asked, turning to Tanner.

"Nothing at all official. A few people are trying to talk me into running, but it's in a couple of years, Sharon. Nothing final. That all right by you?"

"Definitely," she said.

Tanner kept making sure that everyone was coming back for the reception at Shalimar. "We've got tents put up all over the back lawn, so come and fill them," he told them. They all listened.

Two hours later Sharon got to sit down and survey the scene for the first time. The tables were loaded with food made by cousins, aunts, uncles—everyone who cooked or preserved or grew anything and wanted to contribute to the party.

The band had swollen to include a fiddle and a bass somehow, and a lot of people were dancing. Paul was sitting nearby, taking a break, dangling his new daughter on his knee

180   *Kisses Worth Waiting For*

while Kay was out on the dance floor with a bouncing, exuberant Buddy.

Watching them, Sharon leaned against Tanner and smiled. "This is perfect, Tanner. I hope you feel the same way."

"Hey, now that I can take that blasted tie off, anything else would be perfect, Rose." She'd allowed him to call her that, softly, when they were alone, or at least out of hearing of others. He leaned over to the bucket of ice and swirled the champagne bottle. "Have you actually had any of this to drink?"

Sharon shook her head. "Every time I start eating or drinking something, some cousin or another comes by to talk, I set it down, and—poof!—it vanishes by the time I reach for it again."

"Then allow me, Mrs. Williams," he said, pouring her a glass. He lifted it to her lips, watching her while she drank.

"Can I offer you the same?" It was an interesting thought to consider the silver goblet, warmed by Tanner's drinking from it, held in her hand. The reality was even better. Watching his eyes over the rim filled places of Sharon she hadn't even known were empty.

Kisses Worth Waiting For   181

"How much longer do we politely stay?" he murmured in her ear, setting off a ripple of goose bumps down the entire right side of her body.

"About twenty, twenty-five minutes, I'd guess," she said.

"Then I want a dance or two more before we go." He helped her up and led her to the dance floor, cleared on the stone patio of the backyard of the old Victorian house.

When Sharon had walked around it nearly a year ago, considering it for her business, she'd thought of having parties out here. But she'd thought they were going to be business parties, things to launch a client into business, or get-togethers held for sales promotions. She hadn't dreamed that the first big party she'd hold on the grounds of Shalimar, Incorporated, would be her own wedding reception, but somehow it seemed fitting. This old house had brought her and Tanner together, held them like a caress, forced them again and again to face each other until they finally came together today for good.

Her thoughts shifted back to Tanner, who held her in his arms. He'd discarded his coat and tie and looked almost unbearably handsome in the white ruffled shirt, unbuttoned

182   *Kisses Worth Waiting For*

a little, and the sleek gray-striped trousers. "I think we can slip off now, and no one will complain, Tanner. Just make sure none of them follow you, or we'll be shivareed in the middle of the night."

"Shivareed?"

"Yup. Imagine a whole bunch of people with horns and tin pans and loud things yowling outside your bedroom window at three this morning."

"Ouch. I'm glad I had Jim give me his keys and park my own car a few blocks from here."

Sharon made the rounds one last time, giving Anna Mae a few instructions for keeping the office humming for a week, saying good-bye to her parents, and hugging Sarah Beth. "Now be good for India and make sure she's good for you, okay? Keep her company. She's not used to living alone."

"I will. Have a good time and call me while you're gone, okay? I want to see if you think Daddy looks like a bear before his first cup of coffee."

Sharon grinned. "I'll tell you tomorrow, okay?" She hugged her one more time and walked in the wide double doors into the conference room. Tanner was waiting there,

Kisses Worth Waiting For   183

looking out the windows at all the cousins still laughing and talking and dancing.

He took her arm and led her out to Jim's car, looking over his shoulder. "I think the coast is clear," he said out of the side of his mouth. He drove around several blocks, jubilant when he didn't see any cars following them, congratulating himself on evading the followers.

Sharon didn't have the heart to tell him that Paul had pulled her aside when she was leaving and told her he'd persuaded the entire Turner clan to put a moratorium on practical jokes for the newlyweds, and Shane had promised the same for the Mumfords.

They stopped in the driveway of Tanner's house—no, Sharon corrected herself, *their* house. Tanner came around and opened her door and helped her out into the driveway. Then he picked her up over her protests. "Some things were meant to be done traditionally even for people like us, Sharon. I want to carry you over the threshold."

And he did, going up the steps to the front door, unlocking it one-handed, setting her down in the wide hall, then pulling her into his arms again for a long kiss.

184 *Kisses Worth Waiting For*

"This gets better and better," he said. "Apparently marriage agrees with you."

"I hope so, because I plan for it to be a permanent condition."

"Better be careful what you say in front of a future judge. It could be used against you in a court of law," he teased.

"It's already been used in an even higher court, remember. 'For richer, for poorer, in sickness and in health, forsaking all others. . . .' " Sharon's voice caught a little, and she stopped.

"I remember. And I want to remember forever." He took her hand. "Come upstairs with me, Sharon, and I will prove to you that forsaking all others will not be a lonely thing."

The view from the upstairs windows later was lit by a sunset that was nearly perfect. Sharon hoped it would be the one they'd compare sunsets to for twenty or thirty or forty years, trying to find one even more perfect. She doubted if they ever would, but she hoped they'd have plenty of time to try.